From the desk of Emerald Larson, owner and CEO of Emerald, Inc.

To: My personal assistant, Luther Freemont

Re: My newly discovered grandsons,
Caleb Walker, Nick Daniels and Hunter O'Banyon

The time has come to implement the plans I have for my grandsons. You are to take the corporate jet to collect them for a meeting here in Wichita a week from today. Needless to say, I will not tolerate refusals or excuses of any kind. Once I tell my grandsons who they are and what I expect of them, Caleb will be the first to receive his assignment. I already have a man in place at the financial consulting firm to report back to me on his progress. If Caleb is as intelligent and resourceful as I suspect, he should have no trouble taking over the reins of Skerritt and Crowe and turning it into a profitable venture.

As always, I am relying on your complete discretion in this matter.

Emerald Larson

Silhouette Desire is proud to present an exciting new miniseries from

KATHIE DENOSKY

The Illegitimate Heirs

In January 2006—
ENGAGEMENT BETWEEN ENEMIES

In February 2006—
REUNION OF REVENGE

In March 2006—
BETROTHED FOR THE BABY

Dear Reader,

Why not make reading Silhouette Desire every month your New Year's resolution? It's a lot easier—and a heck of a lot more enjoyable—than diet or exercise!

We're starting 2006 off with a bang by launching a brand-new continuity: THE ELLIOTTS. The incomparable Leanne Banks gives us a glimpse into the lives of this high-powered Manhattan family, with *Billionaire's Proposition.* More stories about the Elliotts will follow every month throughout the year.

Also launching this month is Kathie DeNosky's trilogy, THE ILLEGITIMATE HEIRS. Three brothers born on the wrong side of the blanket learned they are destined for riches. The drama begins with *Engagement between Enemies.* *USA TODAY* bestselling author Annette Broadrick is back this month with *The Man Means Business,* a boss/secretary book with a tropical setting and a sensual story line.

Rounding out the month are great stories with heroes to suit your every mood. Roxanne St. Claire gives us a bad boy who needs to atone for *The Sins of His Past.* Michelle Celmer gives us a dedicated physical therapist who is not above making a few late-night *House Calls.* And Barbara Dunlop (who is new to Desire) brings us a sexy cowboy whose kiss is as shocking as a *Thunderbolt over Texas.*

Here's to keeping that New Year's resolution!

Melissa Jeglinski

Melissa Jeglinski
Senior Editor

KATHIE DENOSKY

Engagement Between Enemies

Published by Silhouette Books
America's Publisher of Contemporary Romance

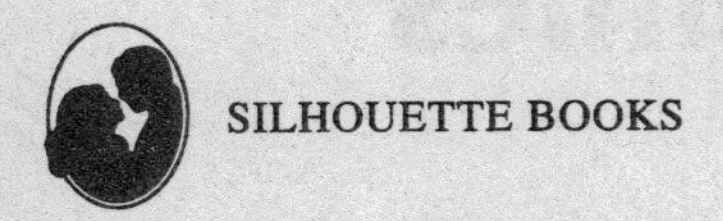

ISBN 0-373-76700-5

ENGAGEMENT BETWEEN ENEMIES

This edition published by arrangement with Harlequin Books S.A.

Visit Silhouette Books at www.eHarlequin.com

Printed in U.S.A.

Books by Kathie DeNosky

Silhouette Desire

Did You Say Married?! #1296
The Rough And Ready Rancher #1355
His Baby Surprise #1374
Maternally Yours #1418
Cassie's Cowboy Daddy #1439
Cowboy Boss #1457
A Lawman in Her Stocking #1475
In Bed with the Enemy #1521
Lonetree Ranchers: Brant #1528
Lonetree Ranchers: Morgan #1540
Lonetree Ranchers: Colt #1551
Remembering One Wild Night #1559
Baby at His *Convenience* #1595
A Rare Sensation #1633
**Engagement between Enemies* #1700

Silhouette Books

Home for the Holidays
"New Year's Baby"

Signature Select

Taken by Storm
"Whirlwind"

*The Illegitimate Heirs

KATHIE DENOSKY

lives in her native southern Illinois with her husband and one very spoiled Jack Russell terrier. She writes highly sensual stories with a generous amount of humor. Kathie's books have appeared on the Waldenbooks bestseller list and received the Write Touch Readers' Award from WisRWA and the National Readers' Choice Award. She enjoys going to rodeos, traveling to research settings for her books and listening to country music. Readers may contact Kathie at: P.O. Box 2064, Herrin, Illinois 62948-5264 or e-mail her at kathie@kathiedenosky.com.

This book is dedicated with deepest appreciation
to Kristi Gold, Roxann Delaney, Mary Gardner
and my editor, Tina Colombo. Without their
encouragement and unwavering support,
this book would not have been possible.

Prologue

Caleb Walker sat at the small round table in the corner of a downtown Wichita, Kansas, hotel bar, staring at the two men seated across from him. Not even the blond waitress giving him an interested smile and the fact that he hadn't had sex in a month of Sundays diverted his attention from the matter at hand.

All of his life, he'd been a man without siblings and with no idea who his father was. But not more than an hour ago, in a plush executive office at the corporate headquarters of Emerald, Inc., all that had changed. Caleb had learned that his father was none other than globe-trotting playboy and heir apparent to the Emerald, Inc. empire, Owen Larson. The late Owen Larson.

Now Caleb was having to come to terms with the fact not only that he knew who his father was, but that the man had gone and gotten himself killed in a boating accident off the coast of France before Caleb had had the chance to confront him for making Caleb's mother pregnant and leaving her without so much as a by-your-leave. He'd also learned that his grandmother was the indomitable Emerald Larson and that the two men sitting across from him were his half brothers.

"I can't believe we've been under that old bat's surveillance all of our lives." A muscle jerked along Hunter O'Banyon's tanned jaw. "She knew everything there was to know about us and didn't do a damned thing to fill us in on the big mystery until now."

"That 'old bat' is our grandmother. And I'd say she's done plenty." Nick Daniels took a swig from the long-necked bottle in his hand, then set it on the table with a thump. "Hiring P.I.s to report our every move from the time we were out of diapers while keeping us in the dark about it takes balls."

"The size of watermelons," Caleb added. His gut still churned with anger that Emerald Larson, founder and CEO of one of the nation's most successful female-owned and operated conglomerates, had denied them all the right to know who they were for so long. "I'm having a problem with her blackmailing our mothers with the threat of cutting us out of inheriting any part of Emerald, Inc. just to keep them silent about her worthless son being the jerk who got them pregnant." He shook his head in disbelief. "I'll give her this much, the old gal's a master at manipulation."

Nick nodded. "I can understand why our moms went along with her. They were hoping to ensure a better life for us. But they paid a hell of a price for it."

"I don't give a damn about inheriting any part of Emerald Larson's little self-made empire." Hunter shook his head. "Hell will freeze over before I dance to her tune."

"So you're going to turn down her offer?" Caleb asked.

If they accepted Emerald's conditions, they'd each be given one of her companies. She'd assured them there were no strings attached and she wouldn't interfere with the way they ran the businesses. But Caleb wasn't fool enough to believe it. It looked like his brothers weren't either.

"I haven't flown a chopper in the past five years." Hunter's mouth thinned to a menacing line. "What business would I have trying to run an air medevac service?"

"Well, it makes more sense than sending a desk jockey to run a cattle ranch in Wyoming." Nick's scowl deepened. "I've lived in a condo in St. Louis for the past twelve years. The closest I get to any kind of livestock these days is the Clydesdales when they pull a beer wagon down Market Street during a parade."

Caleb had to agree that what Emerald Larson was asking them to do was ludicrous. He'd excelled in the business courses he'd taken in high school, but that had been a good number of years ago. He didn't particularly like the idea of making a fool of himself when it became apparent he was in way over his head.

"Well, how do you think I feel?" He shook his head at the thought of what the old gal had in mind for him. "I'm a Tennessee farmer with nothing more than a high-school education. Emerald couldn't have come up with anything more ridiculous than me taking over a financial consulting firm."

Hunter reached for a pretzel from the bowl in the middle of the table. "You can bet that old girl has more up her sleeve than giving us part of Emerald, Inc. out of the goodness of her heart."

"No doubt about it," Nick said, nodding.

Caleb wasn't sure exactly what Emerald Larson had in mind, but he knew just as surely as the sun rose in the east each morning that whatever it was, she'd purposely chosen the business she wanted each of them to run. "It's my guess she wants us to prove something."

Nick looked surprised. "Like what? That we don't know what we're doing?"

"Beats me. But you can bet Emerald Larson has a reason for everything she does." Caleb shrugged as he swallowed the last of his beer. "The way I see it, we have two options. We can either turn the old gal down and walk away, making the sacrifices our mothers made to ensure our futures a total waste of time. Or, we can accept Emerald's offer and show her that she doesn't know beans from buckshot about who we are and where our talents lie."

Hunter looked thoughtful. "I kind of like the idea of showing up the high-and-mighty Mrs. Larson."

"It would serve her right when we all fall on our faces," Nick said, still looking reluctant.

"But if we're going to do this, we at least have to give it our best shot." Caleb stood up and tossed a couple of dollar bills on the table. "It's not in me to do anything half-assed."

"Me neither," the other two said in unison as they rose to their feet and added money to pay for their drinks.

"Then I guess all we have left to do is give Emerald our answer." Caleb suddenly felt as if he was about to step out onto a tightrope without a safety net.

But as he led the way out of the bar and down the street toward the corporate offices of Emerald, Inc., he couldn't help but feel a bit of nervous anticipation begin to build. He'd always enjoyed a challenge. And as unbelievable as it was, he was actually looking forward to taking over Skerritt and Crowe Financial Consultants. His only regret was that he didn't have the education or the slightest idea of how to go about doing the job right.

One

Approaching the reception desk outside the executive offices of Skerritt and Crowe Financial Consultants, Caleb plastered on the professional smile he'd been practicing for the past week. "I'm here to see A. J. Merrick."

"Do you have an appointment, sir?" the older, gray-haired receptionist asked as he started toward the doors behind her desk.

"I'm Caleb Walker." He gave her a conspiratorial wink. "I believe Merrick is expecting me."

"Hold it right there, Mr. Walton," she said, rising to block his way.

"Walker." He frowned. Hadn't Merrick let the other

employees know about his taking over as president of the firm?

The woman shrugged. "Walker, Walton, it doesn't matter what your name is. You're not going in there without an appointment."

Apparently, no one had bothered to inform this woman. "Tell you what—" he glanced at the nameplate on her desk "—Geneva. After I talk with your boss, I promise I'll come back and introduce myself."

"My *boss* is busy and doesn't want to be disturbed." Geneva pointed to a row of chairs lining the wall across the room. "If you'll have a seat, I'll see if I can work you in."

At six feet four inches tall, he towered over the woman by at least a foot, but she wasn't acting the least bit intimidated by it. From the look on her face, she was just as determined to keep him out of the office as he was determined he was going inside.

It was all he could do to keep a straight face. Geneva reminded him of a little banty hen his grandpa used to own—all bluff and ruffled feathers. And if her defiant expression was any indication, he had no doubt that he'd be sitting in the reception area until hell froze over before she picked up the phone and announced his arrival.

"There's no need to go to all that trouble, Geneva." Chuckling, he sidestepped the woman as he reached for the polished knob on the mahogany door with A. J.

Merrick engraved on a brass plaque. "Take my word for it, Merrick is going to want to meet with me right away."

"I'll call security," Geneva threatened, rushing over to the phone.

"You do that," Caleb said, nodding. "I'd like to meet with them, too."

"Oh, you will, buster," she promised, stabbing her finger at the phone's keypad.

Without waiting to see if Geneva reached the security desk, Caleb opened the door and stepped into the spacious office. His gaze immediately zeroed in on the young woman seated behind a huge walnut desk in front of a wall of floor-to-ceiling windows.

With her dark auburn hair pulled back in a bun tight enough to make his grandma Walker proud and a pair of oversize black plastic-framed glasses, she looked more like a headmistress at one of those hoity-toity private all-girl schools in Nashville than a modern corporate secretary. And if her disapproving expression was any indication, she was just as unyielding and strict about rules and protocol as one of those overly uptight teachers, too.

But as he sauntered over to stand in front of the desk, he thought he saw a hint of uncertainty about her—a vulnerability that, considering the image she was obviously trying to project, he hadn't expected. "Excuse me. I'm looking for A. J. Merrick."

"Do you have business here?" she asked, her voice cool enough to freeze ice.

Rising to her feet, she pushed her glasses up her pert little nose with a delicate hand, inadvertently drawing attention to her brilliant blue eyes—eyes that sent him a look that would have probably stopped a lesser man dead in his tracks. It didn't faze Caleb one damned bit. On the contrary. He wasn't sure why, but for some reason he found something quite intriguing about her intense blue gaze.

"I'm—"

"If you're looking for personnel, it's down the hall," she said, cutting him off before he had a chance to introduce himself. Pausing, she arched one perfectly shaped eyebrow. "Was Mrs. Wallace at her desk?"

The woman's no-nonsense tone couldn't quite mask the soft, melodic quality of her voice and had Caleb wondering why the sound seemed to bring every one of his male hormones to full alert. Wondering what the hell had gotten into him, he decided it had to be the fact that he hadn't been with a woman in the better part of a year. That alone was enough to make any normal, healthy adult male feel as though he was about to jump out of his own skin. It also made him overly conscious of every move a woman—any woman—made.

Satisfied that he'd come up with an explanation for his interest in the less-than-friendly secretary, he jerked his thumb over his shoulder. "As far as I know, Geneva's still out there." He chuckled. "Although I'm not real sure she didn't break one of her fingers punching in the number for security."

"Good."

"Good that she might have broken a finger? Or good that she was calling security?" he asked, grinning.

"I didn't mean—" Frowning, she stopped short and it was clear that for a split second, he'd thrown her off guard. "Good that she's summoning security, of course."

"Hey, lighten up. Life is too short to be so uptight."

The woman rounded the end of the desk, her expression anything but welcoming. "I don't know who you think you are or why you're here, but you can't just walk in and—"

The sound of the door crashing against the wall stopped the young woman in midsentence.

"That's him."

Caleb glanced over his shoulder to see the receptionist charge into the office with a defiant glare. Two middle-aged, potbellied uniformed men followed close behind.

"I see you got hold of the security guards, Geneva." He glanced at his watch, then nodded his approval. "Their response time wasn't bad, but I think we could work on improving it, don't you?"

Geneva managed to look down her nose at him despite the difference in their heights, then turned her attention to the woman with the remarkable baby blues. "I'm sorry, Ms. Merrick." She eyed Caleb like she didn't think his elevator went all the way to the top floor. "*He* wouldn't take no for an answer."

Caleb raised an eyebrow. This was A. J. Merrick?

Interesting. She definitely wasn't what he'd expected. Emerald had led him to believe that Merrick was a stodgy old gent, not a twentysomething woman with incredible blue eyes.

As they stared at each other like opponents in a boxing ring, his neglected libido noticed that A. J. Merrick wasn't dressed like most women her age. Instead of her black suit caressing her body and showing off her assets, it hung from her small frame like an empty tow sack. But if her delicate hands, slender neck and what he could see of her long, perfectly shaped legs were any indication, he'd bet his grandpa's best coonhound she was hiding some pretty incredible curves inside all that baggy black linen.

"It's all right, Mrs. Wallace." Ms. Merrick treated Caleb to a triumphant smile that did strange things to his insides and made him feel as if the temperature in the room had suddenly gone up ten degrees. "I'm sure you'll understand that applying for a job now would be a waste of time for both of us." To the guards coming to stand on either side of him, she added, "Please show this gentleman to the parking lot."

"That's mighty unfriendly of you," Caleb said, shaking his head.

Allowing the men to demonstrate how they would

handle the situation if he'd been a real threat, Caleb almost laughed out loud when they clumsily grabbed his arms and attempted to pull them behind his back. He immediately decided that they not only needed to work on their response time to a situation, but could both benefit from a refresher course in methods of restraint. If he'd been of a mind to, he could have broken their hold without doing much more than flexing his biceps.

"I'm not here to apply for a job." He smiled. "I already work here."

"Oh, really?" Ms. Merrick tilted her head curiously. "Since I do the final interviews for all new employees, would you care to refresh my memory and tell me what your name is, when we hired you and just which area of Skerritt and Crowe you think you work in?"

"I got the job a week ago and I intend to work in the office next to yours." Chuckling, he decided he was going to enjoy sparring with A. J. Merrick. "The name is Walker. Caleb Walker."

He could tell from the widening of her baby blues behind those ridiculous glasses that his answers were *not* what she'd expected. But she quickly recovered her composure and motioned toward the two guards. "Mr. Norton, Mr. Clay, please release Mr. Walker immediately."

"But Ms. Merrick—"

"I said, let him go," she repeated. She lifted her stubborn little chin a notch. "Mr. Walker is the new president of Skerritt and Crowe."

From somewhere behind him, he heard Geneva gasp at the same time as the two guards dropped their hold on him.

"Sorry about that, Mr. Walker," one of the men said, clumsily trying to straighten Caleb's shirtsleeve.

Silence reigned for several tense seconds as Caleb and the woman in front of him stared at each other. In a lot of ways she reminded him of another woman and another time.

He took a deep breath. That had been a while back and he'd learned a lot in the few years since. He was no longer a naive farm boy with lofty dreams and a trusting heart. He was a grown man who'd learned his lessons well.

"If you'd give Ms. Merrick and me a few minutes, I'd surely appreciate it," he finally said as he continued to meet her intense gaze. When he heard the quiet click of the door being pulled shut behind the three, Caleb smiled. "What do you say we start over?" He stuck out his hand. "I'm Caleb Walker. It's nice to meet you, Ms. Merrick."

When she hesitantly placed her hand in his, the feel of her soft palm against his sent a shock wave all the way to his toes. She apparently felt the same jolt of electric current because she dropped his hand faster than the high-school football captain's pants hit the floor on prom night. He barely managed to keep from laughing out loud.

"I know I'm earlier than you all expected, but don't you think it would have been a good idea to inform the employees about me? After all, Emerald Larson called you several days ago to tell you I'd be here at the end of this week."

"Mrs. Larson indicated that you'd be here on Friday."

"I'm only a day early," he said, breathing a bit easier when A.J. didn't refer to Emerald as his grandmother.

He'd purposely asked Emerald not to mention their relationship when she called Skerritt and Crowe, and it appeared that she'd respected his wishes. He didn't want or need the added prejudices of being the owner's grandson when he took over.

"It was my intention to introduce you to everyone tomorrow at the directors' meeting," she said, sounding extremely efficient.

"Well, I can guarantee you the cat's out of the bag now," he said, grinning. "I'll bet Geneva and her two sidekicks are spreading the word like fire through a hay field."

To his amazement, she didn't even crack a smile. "I'm sure they are."

Her calm demeanor had Caleb wondering if A. J. Merrick ever let herself lose control. Something told him that it didn't happen often. But he also sensed that when she did let go, it would be a hell of a sight. What he couldn't figure out was why he'd like to be there to see it when she did.

She waved her hand at one of the burgundy leather armchairs in front of her desk. "Please have a seat, Mr. Walker."

Sitting down, he watched her walk around the desk to lower herself into the high-backed executive chair. "Since we're going to be working together, why don't we ditch the formalities?" he asked, wondering what made A. J. Merrick tick. "Call me Caleb."

"I'd rather not, Mr. Walker," she said, straightening some papers on her desk.

"Why not?" He wasn't at all surprised by her insistence on formalities. However, he was dismayed by his own persistence in getting her to let down her guard.

She stopped fussing with the documents to give him a pointed look. "It will only complicate things when the time comes for you to let me go."

Now where had that come from? To his knowledge, he hadn't given her any reason to feel threatened or to believe he'd be firing her, or anyone else for that matter. But she was acting like it was a done deal.

He sat forward. "Where did you get the harebrained idea that I'd be letting you go?"

"Any time there's a change in upper management, the result is always the same. The new president or CEO brings in his or her own people for the top positions and the old regime is history." She shrugged one slender shoulder as she met his gaze head-on. "Since I'm the operations manager over all the departments here at

Skerritt and Crowe, mine will be one of the first heads to roll."

He wasn't sure, but he thought he detected a slight tremor in her voice. But as she continued to stare at him like he was lower than the stuff he scraped off his boots after a trip through the barnyard, he decided he'd imagined the sound. A. J. Merrick was way too professional to show the slightest bit of emotion. What shocked him more than her steely control was his sudden desire to see what lay beneath that cool facade, to discover what she was so obviously trying to hide.

"Let me put your fears to rest right here and now. I'm not getting rid of you or anyone else," he said, forcing his mind back to the matter at hand. She had no way of knowing, and he wasn't about to tell her that he didn't have a clue about running a firm of financial consultants or that he'd have to rely heavily on her and others' experience in order to keep from falling on his face. "Your job is just as safe today as it was before Emerald, Inc. bought this firm."

She pushed her glasses back up her nose with a brush of her hand. "You say that now, but it's a well-known fact that within six months of any takeover there's always a shake-up."

"That might happen with a hostile buyout, but Emerald Larson bought this company with Frank Skerritt and Martin Crowe's blessings. They both wanted to retire, but neither of them had family members who wanted to take the reins of the firm."

As he watched her nibble on her lower lip while she considered his words, he found himself wondering if her perfectly shaped lips were as soft and sweet as they looked. Swallowing hard, he decided that he'd better keep his mind on business and off the fact that Ms. Merrick had the most kissable mouth he'd seen in a very long time.

"I'll be—" he stopped to clear the rust from his throat before he continued "—making a few small changes here and there. But as far as I'm concerned, the only way any of the employees will lose their job is if they up and quit."

"We'll see," she said softly.

Her expression was completely neutral and gave no indication of what she was thinking. But Caleb knew she wasn't buying his assurances for a minute.

Deciding that he'd probably have more luck convincing a pack of wolves to become vegetarians than he would getting A. J. Merrick to believe her job was secure, Caleb took a deep breath and stood up. "I think I'll mosey on out of here and introduce myself to a few of our people."

"But what about the meeting I have set up for tomorrow morning at ten, Mr. Walker?" she asked as she rose from her chair.

Was that a hint of panic he detected in her wide blue eyes?

Interesting. It appeared that any break with tradition threw A. J. Merrick for a loop. He'd have to remember that.

"The name's Caleb." He shrugged. "The meeting is still on. I'll just use it to outline a few of the policy changes I intend to make and explain my plan of action."

He noticed the white-knuckled grip she had on her ink pen and, without thinking, reached across the desk to place his hand on hers in a reassuring manner. But the moment his palm touched her satiny skin, a charge of electricity zinged up his arm and quickly spread throughout his chest. Her startled gasp told him that she felt it, too.

Quickly moving his hand, he tried to appear nonchalant about the gesture. But considering his insides were still tingling like he'd grabbed hold of a 220-volt wire, that was mighty damned hard.

"Relax, Ms. Merrick," he said, wondering what the hell had gotten into him. Surely he didn't need to get laid so badly that he'd started getting turned on by merely touching a woman's hand. "Not only do you have my word that your job's safe, I promise that what I have in mind will improve employee morale and increase productivity."

At least, that's what he hoped to accomplish. Considering he didn't know beans from buckshot about running this or any other company, he'd just have to operate on the trial-and-error system, refer to the management manual he'd picked up at a bookstore and hope for the best.

She defensively folded her arms beneath her breasts and simply stared at him. "I suppose I'll have to take your word on that."

"I guess you will," he said, walking toward the door. He needed to put some distance between them in order to regain his perspective. He was here to take over the consulting firm, not try to figure out why this woman's reluctance to believe him bothered the hell out of him. Or why he was starting to get turned on by staring into her pretty blue eyes. "I'll see you tomorrow morning, Ms. Merrick."

"C-Caleb?" She stumbled over his name, but the sound of it on her soft voice did a real number on his neglected hormones.

His hand on the doorknob, he turned back to face her. "Yes, Ms. Merrick?"

"I suppose since you insist that I use your first name, you might as well call me A.J."

"Okay, A.J." He smiled. Maybe they were making progress after all. "I'll see you first thing in the morning."

A.J. watched the door close behind Caleb Walker a moment before her trembling legs folded and she collapsed into her leather executive chair. Why was her heart racing? And why did her skin still tingle from his touch?

She removed her glasses and buried her face in her hands. What on earth had come over her? She never had been, nor would ever be the type of woman who let a handsome man divert her attention from what was important. At least not since the fiasco with Wesley Pennington III. He'd taught her a valuable lesson, and one that she couldn't afford to forget—mixing business with pleasure was a fool's game, one that ultimately led to disaster.

Normally, it wasn't even an issue. Since losing her heart, her virginity and her first job due to her naiveté, she'd made it a point to do everything she could to appear as professional as possible. It kept things simple and helped to reinforce her strict policy of keeping coworkers at arm's length. And it had worked well.

Most people, and especially men, were put off by her all-business demeanor and didn't bother taking a second glance at her. And that suited her just fine. But Caleb Walker had not only looked twice, he'd focused his disturbing hazel gaze on her from the moment he'd walked into her office.

A tiny tremor coursed through her. He had a way of looking at her that made her more aware of her femininity than she'd ever been in her life. And that was what made him dangerous.

Shaking her head, she tried not to think about the wild fluttering in her lower stomach that she'd experienced when Caleb had smiled at her, and concentrated on the fact that he was her new boss. He was here to take over Skerritt and Crowe and eventually replace her with one of his own people. And even though he'd assured her that wasn't the case, she knew better. Everything she'd worked to achieve in the past five years was about to go down the drain and she was powerless to stop it.

She put her glasses back on and swiveled the chair

around to stare out the plate-glass windows. Blindly watching the late-June sun bathe downtown Albuquerque with its warm afternoon rays, she fought the urge to cry. She had a feeling that Caleb Walker was going to turn her structured, well-ordered world upside down. And there wasn't a thing she could do to stop him.

There was no telling what kinds of changes he intended to implement or just how quickly he'd decide she was dispensable. And the most upsetting aspect of all was the fact that all she could think about was how intense his hazel eyes were, how his light brown hair hanging low on his forehead made him look more like a rebel than a businessman. And how the combination of his deep baritone and sexy Southern accent made her insides hum.

"Don't be a fool," she muttered, turning back to her desk.

She wasn't interested in Caleb Walker any more than he was interested in her. But as she stared at the documents on her desk, she couldn't stop thinking about how broad his shoulders looked in his chambray shirt, how his jeans fit him like a second skin or how her hand still tingled where he'd touched her.

When a tiny moan of frustration escaped, she quickly stuffed the pile of accounting reports she'd been reviewing into her briefcase, grabbed her purse from the bottom drawer of the desk and headed for the door. "I'll be out of the office for the rest of the day," she told Geneva as she rushed past her.

A.J. didn't wait for the startled receptionist's reaction to her atypical behavior. She didn't have time to worry about that now. She needed to get to her apartment before the cool persona she'd perfected over the years slipped away and she revealed what only her parakeet, Sidney, knew about her.

Alyssa Jane Merrick wasn't the cold, emotionless automaton everyone at Skerritt and Crowe thought her to be. She was a living, breathing woman who collected whimsical figurines, shed buckets of tears over sentimental or touching moments, and feared failure more than anything else.

As she walked across the parking lot, she quickened her steps and trotted the distance to her sensible black sedan. She was less than a split second away from doing one of two things. She was going to either let loose with a scream loud enough to wake the dead or start crying like a baby. Neither one was acceptable behavior for her professional image.

Unlocking the driver's door, she threw her briefcase inside, slid behind the steering wheel and closed her eyes. She counted to ten, then twenty as she struggled with her emotions. For the first time in five years, she was close to losing the tight grip she had always held on herself whenever she was at work. And that was something she simply couldn't afford to let happen.

She had never, nor would she ever allow any of these people to see her lose control. Not only would it be a serious breach of her professionalism, but her late father would come back to haunt her for doing something so typically female.

From the time she'd been old enough to listen, her career-military father had stressed how important it was not to let her enemies see any sign of weakness. And there was no doubt about it, Caleb Walker posed a serious threat to her professional demeanor. But he was also the best-looking enemy she'd ever seen.

Two

"The first thing I want to do this morning is assure all of you that your jobs are secure," Caleb said, addressing the directors and department managers. He made it a point to look directly at A. J. Merrick. "Contrary to standard corporate practice, I have no intention of letting anyone go in favor of bringing in my own people. The only way you're going to lose your job is if *you* make the decision to quit."

The doubt he detected in her blue gaze stated quite clearly that she still didn't believe him. What he couldn't figure out was why it mattered to him that she trust him. If their collective sigh of relief was any indication, the rest of the occupants in the room did. What made her opinion of him so damned important?

Deciding not to dwell on the mystery of why her doubts bothered him, Caleb turned his attention back to outlining his plans for the company. "I've reviewed the quarterly reports for the last fiscal year and although growth is slow, it has been steady." He grinned. "And as my grandpa Walker always said, 'If it ain't broke, don't fix it.' That's why I won't be making changes in the daily operations of the company." *At least not until I can take a few business courses and figure out what the hell I'm doing.*

"I like the way your grandpa thinks," Malcolm Fuller said, nodding.

Caleb chuckled. "I'm glad that meets with your approval, Malcolm." He'd met the older man the day before and they'd instantly hit it off. Malcolm reminded Caleb of Henry Walker, his late grandpa—filled with country wisdom and more than willing to speak his mind.

When Caleb noticed several raised eyebrows and the exchange of curious glances between the other department heads seated at the big oval conference table, he frowned. Apparently all of the employees at Skerritt and Crowe were as unaccustomed to the laid-back, informal approach to management as A. J. Merrick was.

Taking a deep breath, he figured there was no time like the present to shake things up and see how receptive the management team was to the changes he did have planned. "Although I don't intend to adjust the operating procedures, I do plan to make a few improvements to the work atmosphere around here."

"What did you have in mind, Mr. Walker?" Ed Bentley asked, looking more than a little nervous.

"The first thing we're going to do is drop the formalities." Caleb gave them all a smile he hoped would put their minds at ease. "Don't you think it's pretty silly to work with someone eight hours a day, day in and day out and not use their given name?" Before they could react, he went on. "We'll naturally continue to give our clients the respect they deserve and address them in a formal manner. But I want you all to feel free to be on a first-name basis with me, as well as each other."

The men and women at the table began to smile. Everyone, except A.J. Her clasped hands resting on the table in front of her had tightened into a white-knuckled knot, indicating that she strongly disagreed with his decision.

Why would she object to doing away with an outdated tradition? Hadn't she learned in college that a more relaxed environment encouraged teamwork and raised productivity? Hell, he'd found that little tidbit of information on the Internet, so it couldn't be that big a secret.

"You want us to call you Caleb?" Maria Santos asked hesitantly.

Grinning, he turned his attention to the director of the payroll department. "That's my name, Maria."

"What other changes do you have planned...Caleb?" one of the other men asked.

"Effective immediately, there's an open-door policy

between upper management and the workers on the floor." He paused to let them digest his statement. "I want every employee we have, no matter what their position, to feel comfortable with bringing problems and complaints to our attention, as well as sharing ways to improve morale and bring in new clients."

"You've got a lot of good ideas," Joel McIntyre, the head of the billing department, said, nodding his approval. "Is there anything else?"

"As a matter of fact there is, Joel." Caleb smiled. He was sure the last couple of changes he was about to announce would be welcomed by everyone, including A. J. Merrick. "Since most of our business is conducted over the phone and through the Internet, I don't see any reason why we can't relax the dress code around here. I'll still expect you to dress accordingly when you meet with one of our clients, but from now on you're all free to wear whatever you like." He chuckled. "That is, as long as it's decent and doesn't look like something you'd put on to clean out the barn."

He laughed out loud when several of the men immediately reached up to remove their ties and unfasten the top button of their shirts. "I guess this means everyone is in favor of doing away with the dress code."

When he glanced at A.J. his smile faded. *Well, almost everyone.*

"Is that all?" she asked tightly. She stared straight at him and it was as clear as a cloudless sky that she wasn't happy.

None of the other department heads seemed to notice that the operations manager was even in the same room with them, let alone less than enthusiastic about his ideas. But Caleb had been aware of her presence from the moment she'd sat down in the chair at the far end of the conference table. He'd hoped that once she heard what he had planned she'd find his ideas to be innovative or at least be open to giving them a chance.

Unfortunately, she looked even more unhappy than she had yesterday afternoon when he'd walked into her office and announced who he was. But more troubling than her lack of enthusiasm was his reaction to her reluctance. He had an almost uncontrollable urge to walk over to her, take her in his arms and reassure her that the changes he planned to make would be of benefit to everyone.

He shook his head, as much to dispel his disturbing thoughts as to let her know he had more plans in the works. "I have one more announcement before I let you all get back to work." Tearing his gaze from A.J., he forced his attention to the others seated around the table. "On Monday, there will be a seminar for all managers to learn team-building techniques. Then, once a month, the firm will pick up the tab for you and all of the people in your department to take a Friday off and put what you've learned into action."

"This is where we go on picnics, play golf and things like that to build communication skills and encourage interaction with our coworkers, isn't it?" Joel asked, sounding excited by the possibilities.

"That's the plan," Caleb said, nodding. At least others could see his objective, even if A.J. couldn't. "There's no reason we can't have fun while we develop a tight, efficient team." Smiling, he pushed his chair back and rose to his feet. He'd given them enough to digest for one day. In the next week or so, he'd shake things up a little more. "Now, what do you say we all get back to work and make some money."

As the meeting broke up and her coworkers surrounded Caleb to express their enthusiasm for the changes he'd be making, A.J. escaped to the sanctuary of her office. Closing the door behind her, she leaned up against it as she struggled to breathe. She felt as if she were about to suffocate on the myriad of emotions racing through her. In less than an hour, Caleb Walker had single-handedly destroyed every reason she had for working at Skerritt and Crowe. And he didn't even realize it.

He thought he was doing everyone a favor by improving the quality of their work atmosphere. And she had to admit that what he planned would probably motivate the employees and breathe new life into the firm.

But she'd purposely chosen to accept the position

with Skerritt and Crowe, instead of at a more modern financial group, because of the formalities and old-fashioned approach to management. It enabled her to focus all of her attention on her job and kept the people she worked with at a safe distance.

Pushing away from the door, she walked around her desk and sank into the high-backed leather chair. Although she wasn't antisocial by nature, she'd learned the hard way to keep her coworkers at arm's length. It was the only sure way to guard herself against betrayal and the emotional pain that accompanied it.

But what frustrated and confused her more than anything else was her reaction to Caleb. The entire time he'd been outlining the ways he intended to destroy her safety net, all she'd been able to think about was how handsome he was and how his deep Southern drawl made her insides hum.

Barely resisting the urge to let loose with a scream that was sure to send Geneva Wallace into cardiac arrest, A.J. turned to her computer screen and opened the file containing her résumé. There was no longer any question about it. Her days as operations manager at Skerritt and Crowe were numbered and she'd do well to start looking for another job.

"A.J., could you come in here?" Caleb's voice invading her office through the intercom caused her stomach to flutter wildly. "I have something I need to talk over with you."

What could he possibly want now? Hadn't he done enough in the past hour to turn her world upside down?

Sighing, she depressed the talk button. "I'm working on something at the moment. Could we postpone the discussion until this afternoon?" He didn't need to know that she was updating her résumé or that she planned on finding another job. When silence reigned, she pushed the button again. "Mr. Walker? Caleb?"

She gasped when the door connecting their offices opened and he strolled into the room.

"Sorry if I startled you, but I'm a face-to-face kind of guy," he said, grinning. "I like to look a person in the eye when I'm talking to them."

The sound of his voice and his sexy grin sent a shiver streaking up her spine and had her wondering what else he liked to do face-to-face. Her breath caught and she did her best to hide her shock at the direction her wayward thoughts had taken.

"What did you want to discuss, Mr.—"

He raised one dark eyebrow at the same time he cleared his throat.

Resigned, she closed the computer file containing her résumé. "What did you want to discuss…Caleb?"

He smiled his approval. "I think I've come across another way to improve employee morale."

Just what she wanted to hear, she thought disgustedly, another cockamamy idea that would no doubt increase her anxiety level.

She trained her gaze on his forehead to keep from looking directly into his startling hazel eyes. "What did you have in mind?"

"I'm thinking about turning the break room into a 'family room.'"

A.J.'s mouth dropped open and her gaze flew to his. "Excuse me?"

"Better watch that." He chuckled. "You might catch a fly."

She snapped her mouth shut. Didn't he take anything seriously?

"Would you care to explain what you mean when you use the term *family room?*" she asked, rubbing at the sudden pounding in her temples.

"I'm thinking couches, coffee tables and a big-screen TV," he said, looking thoughtful. "When our employees take their breaks, they should be able to relax and enjoy the few minutes they have away from the job."

"If you make it too comfortable, they'll go to sleep," A.J. said before she could stop herself.

She hadn't meant to be so blunt. But facts were facts and he might as well be aware of them right up front.

He grinned. "Nothing wrong with a little power nap now and then. Studies have shown that it gives most people a second wind."

She'd seen the research and couldn't argue with the findings, but that didn't mean she agreed with them.

"Are you wanting to know what I think of the idea?" she asked cautiously.

"Not really." He gave her a smile that warmed her all the way to her toes. "But I would like your help putting the project into action."

Her first inclination was to refuse his request. But to her amazement, she found herself asking, "What do you want me to do?"

"I'd really appreciate your input on what colors and style of furniture to use." His expression turned sheepish. "I'm not real up on this decorating stuff."

Oh, he was good. He knew just when to turn up the wattage on that smile and use his boyish charm to get exactly what he wanted. Fortunately, she was immune to such tactics.

"What makes you think I'm any better?"

"I don't." He shrugged. "But I need a woman's perspective. The room needs to be comfortable for both men and women. If I try to do it entirely on my own, it'll end up looking like a sports bar."

"Why don't you get Mrs. Wallace to help you?" A.J. hedged. "I've heard her say she never misses that television show where friends redecorate each other's rooms."

"I have Geneva busy heading up another project," he said, grinning.

"You do?" Good Lord, what on earth had he charmed their stodgy sixty-year-old secretary into doing?

"I've given her a five-thousand-dollar budget for uniforms and equipment and put her in charge of organizing our sports teams."

A.J. couldn't believe what she was hearing. "You've got to be joking."

"Nope." His smile intensified. "Depending on the amount of interest among the employees, we're going to have bowling and volleyball teams this winter and a softball team next summer."

"You do realize this consulting firm is comprised of accountants and financial analysts, don't you?" She shook her head in disbelief. "That's not exactly the material jocks are made of."

He shook his head. "I don't care if we have winning teams. I'm more interested in creating an overall sense of unity among the employees." Rising to his feet, he stretched and started walking toward the door to his office. "You've got the weekend to give some thought to what we can do to the break room, then we'll go over your ideas next week."

As she watched him close the door behind himself, A.J. groaned. From the time she'd been old enough to understand, her father had preached the military mantra of structure and order. He'd said they were essential for a successful life. Captain John T. Merrick had believed it, had lived by it and had insisted that his daughter adhere to it. He'd even chosen the boarding school she'd attended after the death of her mother because of its strict code of conduct and rigid set of rules. And the one and only time she'd deviated from the path her father had set her on, she'd ended up in the middle of a humiliating workplace scandal.

But she'd survived because that's what her late father would have expected her to do. It had been extremely difficult, but she'd picked up the pieces of her shattered pride, became a born-again virgin and found her present job at Skerritt and Crowe. And she'd been—if not happy—content for the past five years.

Unfortunately, it seemed that contentment had come to an end with the arrival of Caleb Walker. When he'd strolled into her office yesterday afternoon with his good-old-boy attitude and devastating good looks to announce he was taking over the firm, she felt as if she'd been tossed into a vortex. He represented everything in life she'd been taught to approach with caution, if not avoid altogether. He was innovative in the way he approached management and his ideas were unorthodox and, unless she'd missed her guess, for the most part spontaneous.

So why did her pulse pound and air feel as if it were in short supply whenever they were in the same room? Why did his sexy Southern drawl send sparks of electric current over every nerve in her body? And why did the sight of his wide shoulders and slender hips cause her body to hum with a restlessness like she'd never known before?

Biting her lower lip to stop its trembling, she hastily reopened the computer file containing her résumé. There was absolutely no question about the matter. She had to find another job as soon as possible or risk losing what little sense she had left.

The following Tuesday afternoon, Caleb sat at his desk, wondering what on God's green earth Emerald Larson had gotten him into. He didn't have the vaguest idea of how he was supposed to deal with one of Skerritt and Crowe's best clients. His night classes at the University of New Mexico weren't scheduled to start until the end of next month. He somehow doubted the business administration courses he'd signed up for would start out covering the interaction with clientele, anyway.

He drummed his fingertips on the desk's polished surface. He hadn't been able to find anything on conducting meetings with clients in the management manual, either. The damned thing only covered supervising employees and ways to improve their work environment. It was completely useless for learning how to deal with clients.

But whether Caleb knew what he was doing or not, it didn't change the fact that Raul Ortiz wanted to meet with him. Caleb had taken over running the financial consulting firm that had helped Ortiz Industries create one of the best employee investment plans in the state, and he suspected that Ortiz wanted to make sure Caleb passed muster.

When he heard A.J.'s voice through the door connecting their offices, Caleb's spirits lifted. The woman might be driving him crazy trying to figure out what made her tick, but he'd read her personnel file. She really knew her stuff when it came to financial planning and marketing analysis. He'd also discovered that she'd graduated from high school at the age of fifteen and had acquired her master's degree in investment banking and business administration by the time she was twenty.

If he took her with him when he drove down to Roswell, surely the meeting with Ortiz would work out. He was good with people and A.J. was a whiz at anything to do with accounting and financial planning. Together they should make a hell of a team.

Caleb took a deep breath and rose to his feet. He hated feeling inadequate at anything. But he had decided up front that he was going to have to rely on the people working for him until he took courses and got a basic understanding of the business Emerald had given him. It looked as though that reliance was going to have to start sooner than later.

Opening the door between their offices, he smiled when A.J. glanced at him over the top of her computer screen. "I just got a call from a man down in Roswell," he said, walking over to slump into the chair in front of her desk. "He claims to be our most satisfied client."

"That would be Mr. Ortiz," she answered, nodding. "He's one of our most valued patrons."

"That's what he said." Caleb chuckled. "I get the idea he's also one of our most outspoken clients."

"I've never known him to mince words," she said, pushing her glasses up her pert little nose. The action drew attention to her remarkable eyes and Caleb had to remind himself that he'd entered her office for a reason other than staring into her baby blues.

"So you've dealt with him before?"

She nodded. "Mr. Skerritt took care of Ortiz Industries' employee investment program, but he assigned me to advise Mr. Ortiz on his own personal retirement package. Why do you ask?"

"He wants me to drive down to Roswell tomorrow for a get-acquainted meeting." Trying to sound nonchalant, Caleb added, "I've decided I'll take you with me."

"Me?" Her eyes widened behind her oversize glasses and the panic he saw in their depths reminded him of a deer caught in the headlights of a car. Was the thought of spending time with him that upsetting?

"Is there a problem, A.J.?"

"Why? I mean, I can't possibly—" She suddenly closed her mouth and simply stared at him.

As he returned her gaze, Caleb did his best to keep his attention on the issue at hand and off her perfectly shaped lips. "I realize this is on the spur of the moment, but I don't see that we have any other choice. Since I've just taken over here, I don't know diddly-squat about Ortiz or our business with him. And until I'm up to speed on the individual accounts of our clients, I'd rather not run the risk of losing them."

His argument made sense to him. He just hoped it sounded reasonable to her.

Watching her nibble on her lower lip as she mulled over what he'd said, it was all he could do to keep from groaning. Why did he suddenly find her mouth so damned fascinating? Hadn't he learned a damn thing about professional, career-minded women?

"What time is the meeting?" she asked.

Was it his imagination or was there a slight tremor in her voice?

"Ortiz wants to give me a tour of the manufacturing plant tomorrow afternoon, then have dinner around six or seven."

"It would be too late for us to drive back tomorrow evening and I have two phone meetings early the next morning." She sounded extremely relieved when she added, "I'm sorry, but I really think my going with you would be impossible. We've been courting these potential clients for several months and there's the possibility of losing them if I reschedule the calls."

He wasn't about to give up that easily. "Where are they located?"

"Mr. Sanchez is in Las Cruces and Mrs. Bailey is in Truth or Consequences." Her eyes narrowed. "Why?"

"If I remember my high-school geography, those two places aren't that far from Roswell," he said, thinking fast. "Call and tell them we'll be in their area day after tomorrow and that we'd like to meet with them in person. It'll show that we'd really like to work for them, as well as free you up to go to Roswell with me. Then we'll drive back after dinner Thursday evening." Deciding to beat a hasty retreat before she could find another excuse, he headed for the door. "I'll come by your place around ten in the morning."

"Th-that won't be necessary," she said, stopping him. When he turned back, she added, "I have to come in tomorrow morning to tie up a few loose ends. We can leave from here."

Caleb could tell she wasn't happy, but that couldn't be helped. He wasn't particularly proud of having to rely on her expertise to keep from looking like a fool in front of a client.

"Fair enough," he said, nodding. "I'll have Geneva make a reservation for tomorrow night in Roswell."

"That should be reservations—plural—as in two rooms."

"Of course."

Heading out the door to speak with their secretary, Caleb couldn't help but grin. He clearly made A. J. Merrick as nervous as the parents of a four-year-old talking to the preacher after Sunday services.

The next two days had the potential to prove extremely interesting and in a way he hadn't counted on. Not only would he get to see how A.J. dealt with clients, he had a feeling he just might see that cool self-control of hers slip, as well.

Three

After an uneventful drive down to Roswell, a tour of Ortiz Industries and a highly successful dinner meeting with Mr. Ortiz, all A.J. wanted was the solitude of her motel room and a nice, hot, relaxing bath. Thoroughly exhausted from tossing and turning the night before, she'd spent the entire day in Caleb's disturbing presence and she was more than ready to put a bit of distance between them.

"Why don't you check in for us while I get the bags from the back of the truck?" he asked as he stopped the pickup in front of the motel entrance.

She opened the passenger side door. "I assume the rooms are under the firm's name?"

"Yep. Geneva said she reserved the last two rooms

in Ros—" He stopped abruptly when a family of glow-in-the-dark aliens with oval-shaped heads and big, unblinking eyes walked past the front of the truck and got into a blue minivan.

"This is festival week," A.J. explained. She couldn't help but laugh at the incredulous expression on his handsome face. "You'll probably see a lot of that sort of thing."

"I saw the banners when we drove through town." He shook his head. "But I didn't realize they went to extremes with the alien thing."

Getting out of the truck, she nodded. "It's the anniversary of the Roswell Incident. People from all over the world converge on the town the first part of July to attend seminars, share the experiences they've had with extraterrestrials and participate in a variety of activities, including a costume contest."

Caleb chuckled when another alien, this one with tentacles and silver eyes, waved as he drove past in a yellow Volkswagen Beetle. "Sounds like we're lucky Geneva found rooms for us."

"I'm really surprised she did on such short notice."

A.J. closed the truck door and, breathing a sigh of relief that she'd soon have a little time to herself, entered the motel lobby and approached the desk clerk. "I'm with Skerritt and Crowe Financial Consultants. I believe you have a couple of rooms for us."

The smiling teenage girl behind the counter snapped her gum, then blew a bubble as she checked her computer screen. “Actually, we have you down for one room with a couple of beds.”

“There must be a mistake,” A.J. said, shaking her head. She knew Geneva Wallace was far too capable to make that big of an error. “Could you please double-check the reservations?”

Shrugging, the girl keyed in the information again. A moment later, she looked up, shaking her head. “It shows only one room reserved for the Skerritt and Crowe folks. But like I said, it does have two beds.”

A.J.’s temples began to throb. “Do you have another room available?”

The girl smiled apologetically. “Sorry. This week’s been booked solid for months. In fact, if we hadn’t had a late cancellation, we wouldn’t have had this room for you.” Snapping her gum, she looked thoughtful. “I’d say the closest motel with rooms available would probably be down in Artesia. And that’s real iffy.”

“Is there a problem?” Caleb asked, walking up to stand beside A.J.

“Apparently there’s been a mix-up and they only have one room for us.” She suddenly knew how Dorothy must have felt when the tornado picked her up and she came over the rainbow, crashing down in the land of Oz. “With the festival going on there aren’t any rooms available for miles. It looks like we’ll have to drive on to Las Cruces tonight.”

To her astonishment, Caleb shook his head. “It’s already dark, we're both tired and some of the roads between here and there are two-lanes. Driving in unfamiliar territory under those conditions wouldn't be a good idea."

Desperation began to claw at her insides. Had he lost his mind?

"We can't stay in the same room."

"You can have the bed and I'll sleep on the floor." He made it sound so logical.

"The room has two double beds," the teenage girl spoke up helpfully.

"We'll take it," he said, setting their overnight cases down to reach for his wallet.

If she thought she'd felt desperate before, A.J. was a hairbreadth away from an all-out panic attack. Tugging on his arm, she led him over to the seating area of the lobby for a private discussion.

"You can't be serious."

"We don't have a choice."

"What happens when the employees at the firm find out that we spent the night in the same room?"

He shook his head. "Unless one of us tells them, they'll never know."

"Don't fool yourself. What do you think is going to happen when you turn in the receipt to accounts payable?" she asked, knowing that once word got out there was only one room on the bill, the gossip and speculation would run rampant.

"I'll put it on my credit card instead of Skerritt and Crowe's." He sounded so darned reasonable, she wanted to stomp.

"But—"

He reached out and put his hands on her shoulders. "I agree, it's a major pain in the butt that we can't have our own rooms. But we're both adults, A.J. We can handle this." Before she could stop him, he removed his wallet from his hip pocket and handed a credit card to the girl behind the counter.

Her heart did a backflip. Maybe he could deal with the situation, but she wasn't so sure about herself. Spending the entire day with him, first in the close confines of his pickup truck, then in the meeting with Mr. Ortiz, had more than taken its toll.

From the moment they'd left the Skerritt and Crowe offices that morning, her senses had been assaulted by the man. The scent of his woodsy aftershave, the timbre of his deep voice and the occasional brush of his arm against hers when he opened doors for her had charged every cell in her being with a restlessness she refused to define. If she had to spend an entire night in the same room with Caleb only a few feet away, there was a very real possibility she'd be a raving lunatic by morning.

As he sat on the side of the motel bed, Caleb took off his boots, then picked up the television's remote control and absently flipped through the channels. He had to get his mind off the woman changing clothes in the bathroom.

Glancing at the closed door, he shook his head. He'd put in a hell of a day listening to her soft voice and watching her move with a catlike grace that he found absolutely fascinating. But it was the few times they'd brushed against each other that had him feeling like he was about to jump out of his own skin. What was there about A.J. that sent his hormones racing through his blood like the steel balls in an pinball machine?

She was the consummate professional and gave every indication that she was totally immersed in her career. And he'd learned the hard way to avoid her type like a bachelor avoids a widows' convention. So why was she all he'd been able to think about from the moment he'd laid eyes on her? What was there about her that he found so damned compelling?

Her clothes certainly weren't provocative or meant to entice a man. And although she was far from homely, A.J. sure didn't wear makeup or style her hair in a way to make herself look anything but plain.

He frowned. It was as if she was doing everything she possibly could to keep from attracting attention to herself.

That's what he was having the devil of a time trying to figure out. A.J. didn't look or act like an executive. Leslie Ann Turner, the woman he'd been involved with a few years back, had been the perfect example of a corporate climber and taken great pains to look attractive at work, as well as when they'd gone out on the town. They'd met by accident when he'd attended a farm symposium at one of the downtown Nashville hotels and she'd stopped by the lounge after work for drinks with her girlfriends. He'd asked her out and that had started their two-year affair. She'd been a junior executive then and hadn't yet developed a thirst for power and position, nor had she looked down on him because he'd had nothing more than a high-school education.

But as time had gone on and she'd gotten a few promotions under her belt, that had changed. She'd stopped asking him to attend corporate parties with her and had adopted the attitude that the measure of a man was determined by the number of diplomas he held. And it really hadn't come as a big surprise when she'd dumped him like a blind date on a Saturday night.

However, as hard as it had been to face the fact that she apparently thought he wasn't good enough for her, he did have her to thank for a lesson well learned. A career woman wasn't anyone he wanted to become involved with, no matter how compelling her baby blues were.

But A.J. didn't seem to possess the same barracuda instincts, the same do-whatever-it-takes-to-get-ahead attitude that Leslie Ann had. Hell, there were a couple of times when he'd been outlining the policy changes, then later when he'd asked her to help with the break room renovations, that A.J. had almost looked unsure and vulnerable.

As he sat there pondering his uncharacteristic fascination with A.J., the bathroom door opened. Looking up, Caleb's jaw dropped and he felt like he'd been blindsided by a steamroller. With her owlish glasses off and her long, auburn hair down around her shoulders, A. J. Merrick was a knockout.

He swallowed hard as she walked past him to the other bed. Her emerald silk pajamas and robe enhanced the red highlights in her hair and were the perfect contrast to her flawless porcelain complexion and baby-blue eyes.

"The bathroom's all yours," she said with a wave of her delicate hand.

She still hadn't looked his way and he was damned glad. He'd been staring at her like a teenage boy stared at his first glimpse of a *Playboy* centerfold and there was no doubt in his mind that she'd think she was sharing a room with some kind of nutcase.

Suddenly feeling as if the walls were closing in on him, Caleb stood up. "I'm not all that tired," he lied. "I think I'll go down to the restaurant and get a cup of coffee." Edging toward the door, he asked, "Do you want me to bring something back for you?"

"No, thank you."

"Will you be okay here alone?"

She turned her incredible baby blues on him. "Sure. Why do you ask?"

He wasn't about to tell her that she looked prettier

and more feminine than he'd ever imagined. Nor did he want to admit that he felt like a prize jackass for running like a tail-tucked dog.

"Just checking."

She hid a huge yawn with one delicate hand. "I'll probably be asleep before you make it downstairs."

The thought of what she might look like with her long silky hair spread across the pillow, her dark lashes resting on her creamy cheeks like tiny feathers, made his body tighten and had him reaching for the doorknob in less than two seconds.

"Night," she called.

"Uh, yeah, night," he muttered, closing the door behind him. He was halfway down the hall before he realized his boots were still sitting on the floor beside the bed in their room.

He stopped dead in his tracks. "Well, hell."

"Flashback?"

Turning, Caleb found a tall, skinny man, with what looked like a piece of tinfoil molded to his bald head, standing behind him. "Excuse me?"

"I asked if you were having a flashback from your last encounter with *them,*" the man said, pointing toward the ceiling. "Some of us have flashbacks from time to time. Especially if the encounter was a really close one."

When Caleb caught on that the gentleman was referring to E.T., he shook his head. "No. This was more like a first-time sighting."

"I can totally relate. It can be a pretty disconcerting experience the first time you see *them*." Grinning, the man reached up to adjust his foil skullcap. "But as time goes on you'll find yourself looking forward to it and even hoping for an encounter of the third kind."

Caleb nodded. He was already anticipating how soft and feminine A.J. would look when she woke up tomorrow morning. And just the idea of a close encounter with her of any kind made him hard as hell.

When the man continued on down the hall, Caleb turned and walked back toward the room. "You have no idea, buddy. No earthly idea at all."

The moment the door closed behind Caleb, A.J. collapsed onto the side of the motel bed. She'd felt his gaze follow her across the room when she'd walked out of the bathroom and her knees still felt as if they were made of rubber. How on earth would she be able to close her eyes, let alone get a wink of sleep?

All she could think about was what he'd wear to bed and how he'd look first thing in the morning when he woke up. And just knowing that he'd be sleeping a few feet away sent shivers up her spine and made breathing all but impossible.

A.J. glanced around the room in near panic. She needed to get her mind off her disturbing boss. In desperation, she picked up the remote control and switched the television to a classic film channel. It would definitely be in her best interest to try losing herself in the plot of an old movie. Maybe then she'd be able to forget that she was about to spend the night in the same room as the sexiest man she'd ever known.

When she realized the film was *An Affair to Remember,* she took off her robe, pulled back the covers and crawled into bed. Even though she'd seen the movie at least twenty times and always ended up sobbing her heart out, it was one of her all-time favorites.

Settling back against the pillows, she managed to forget about her current situation as she braced herself for the movie's ending. And sure enough, when the hero discovered why the heroine had failed to meet him at the top of the Empire State Building, A.J.'s tears began to fall.

Unfortunately, Caleb chose that very moment to return to the room. "I forgot my—" He stopped abruptly. "Are you crying?"

Mortified that he'd caught her in a less-than-professional moment, she stared at the television screen. "N-no."

To her horror, he walked over to the side of her bed and sat down. "Yes, you are." He took her hands in his. "What's wrong, A.J.?"

"N-nothing." She'd known he'd be returning in a short time. Why on earth had she chosen to watch a movie that never failed to make her cry buckets?

"Look at me, sweetheart." The gentle tone of his voice caused her tears to fall faster. Why wouldn't he just go away and leave her alone?

"I...can't." Dear God, could the day get any worse? It had been years since she'd allowed anyone to see her shed a tear. But here she was crying like a baby. And in front of her new boss, no less. She'd never been more humiliated in her entire life.

Why couldn't he find what he'd forgotten and leave? At least, long enough for her to pull herself together.

He cupped her cheek and turned her head until their gazes met. "I'm sorry, sweetheart. I didn't realize you were this upset by the situation. Please don't cry. I'll sleep in my truck if it will make you feel better."

His sincerity touched her deeply and for reasons she didn't care to analyze, she couldn't allow him to think her emotional display was because they'd be spending the night in the same room. "It's...the movie."

Glancing over his shoulder, he turned back to smile at her a moment before he reached out and took her into his arms. "That one always does a number on my mom, too."

"W-what are you doing?"

"It's all right, Alyssa."

The sound of his deep voice saying her name with such tenderness sent a shock wave straight to her core and she didn't even think to push away from him. "How did you...know my name?"

"It's in your personnel file." He pulled her to him, then smoothed his hands down her back in a comforting manner. "And don't go getting any ideas about me replacing you. I reviewed all of the managers' files."

"Why?" God help her, but with his strong arms wrapped around her and her cheek pressed to his wide chest, she wasn't sure she cared why he was going through hers or anyone else's file.

"I was trying to decide what team-building activities would best serve each manager and their department." His warm breath stirred her hair and sent shivers streaking up her spine. He hugged her close. "Cold?"

Unable to form a coherent sentence, she nodded. Even if she could have found her voice, she wasn't about to tell him the real reason she trembled.

But when he pulled back to look down at her, she knew he wasn't buying her excuse for a minute. "Are you sure?"

With his intense hazel gaze holding her captive, she wasn't sure of her own name, let alone what he'd asked her. "W-what was the question?"

"It doesn't matter, Alyssa." His sexy drawl caused her insides to feel as if they'd been turned to warm pudding and as he slowly lowered his head, she couldn't for the life of her remember why it should.

As his mouth brushed over hers, her heart skipped several beats. She should call a halt to this insanity and send him outside to spend the night in his truck. But for reasons she couldn't begin to explain, she wanted Caleb's kiss, wanted to feel his hard body pressed to her. And when he settled his lips more fully over hers, she threw caution to the wind and melted against him.

As he explored her with a tenderness that stole her breath, tiny electrical impulses skipped over every nerve in her body and she couldn't have stopped him if her life depended on it. Didn't even want to.

His kiss was slow and thoughtful and warm tingles filled her when he traced the seam of her mouth with his tongue. He was asking permission to deepen the kiss and without so much as a thought to the consequences, she parted to give him access to her tender inner recesses.

A heady warmth began to swirl through her veins when he slipped inside to caress and coax her into a response. She knew she was playing with fire, but as he teased her with featherlight strokes, temptation never tasted as good as Caleb's masterful kiss.

When he lowered her to the mattress, her stomach fluttered with the first stirrings of need and her nipples tightened in anticipation at the feel of his hand cupping her breast through the fabric of her silk pajamas. She wanted his hands on her body, wanted to feel his hair-roughened flesh pressed to her sensitive skin.

Tugging at the collar of his shirt, she was startled out of the sensual haze in her addled brain by a feminine moan of frustration. Had that sound really come from her? Dear heavens, what was she doing?

Embarrassed beyond belief, Alyssa pushed against him. "I can't. Please stop."

Caleb looked as dazed as she felt. "It's…all right,

sweetheart." He cleared his throat and sat up. "It stops right here." Rising to his feet, he smiled. "I think I'll go get that cup of coffee. Are you sure I can't bring something back for you?"

It appeared that he was going to act as if nothing had happened between them. Unsure whether she was disappointed or relieved, she decided to take his lead and ignore the fact that they'd been making out like a couple of hormone-crazed teenagers.

She shook her head. "N-no, thank you. I think I'll turn in for the night."

He stared at her for several seconds before he reached down and lifted her chin with his forefinger. "I'll try not to disturb you when I return."

"I sleep pretty sound." His touch was doing strange things to her insides and she sounded as if she'd run a marathon. "I doubt that you'll make enough noise to wake me."

"I didn't say anything about making noise, sweetheart." His deep chuckle and mischievous grin sent her pulse racing. "There's a big difference."

Alyssa felt as if her heart suddenly dropped to her stomach, then bounced back up to pound at her ribs when she realized what he meant. Before she could find her voice, Caleb gave her a quick kiss on the forehead, then picked up his boots and walked across the room and out the door without a backward glance.

Staring at the closed door, she had to force herself to

breathe. Now she knew for certain that she'd landed on the other side of the rainbow. Either that, or she and Caleb had both been taken over by aliens. After all, they were in Roswell, where the unexplained was not only accepted, it was expected.

But as she reached up to turn off the bedside lamp, she shook her head. She knew what had gotten into her and it had nothing whatsoever to do with friends from a faraway galaxy. From the moment Caleb Walker had strolled into her office, she'd fought it, tried to ignore it and even denied its existence. But the truth was, she was attracted to her new boss.

She burrowed deeper into the bed and pulled the covers up to her chin. What on earth was she going to do now?

In the past few minutes, she'd abandoned the two most important rules she'd set for herself. She'd allowed one of her coworkers to witness her emotional side and she'd practically thrown herself at him when he'd offered her comfort.

She sighed heavily. There was no way around it now. Her departure from Skerritt and Crowe was not only inevitable, it was imminent.

Closing her eyes, she tried not to think of the damage she'd done to her professional reputation and willed herself to relax. She probably wouldn't be able to sleep, but at least she wouldn't be sobbing like a baby when Caleb returned this time.

What seemed like only a few minutes later, the ringing phone roused her. Who on earth could be calling at this time of night?

She grumbled about wanting to hurt whoever was on the other end of the line as she switched on the light and snatched up the receiver before it could ring again. "Hello?"

Dead silence greeted her.

"Is someone there?" she asked impatiently.

"Who is it?" Caleb asked, sounding groggy.

She sucked in a sharp breath as she glanced over at the other bed. Apparently she'd been asleep longer than she'd realized. He'd not only returned to their room, but he'd been sleeping as soundly as she'd been.

"Ms. Merrick?"

"Yes." She looked at the digital alarm clock on the nightstand. "Who is this and why are you calling at two in the morning?"

"This is Clarence Norton, A.J.…Ms. Merrick. I'm sorry to wake you," the security guard from Skerritt and Crowe said apologetically. "The motel operator was supposed to connect me with Mr. Walker's room."

"Is there a problem?"

"The firm's silent alarm went off at the police station about an hour ago," he explained. "They called me to come down and let them in so they could do a thorough search of the building."

Fully awake, she asked, "Was there a break-in?"

"No," Clarence assured her. "But the alarm system shorted out and—"

"What's going on?" Caleb threw back the sheet and sat up on the side of the bed. "Give me the phone."

Alyssa held up her finger to silence him, but it was too late. Clarence had already heard Caleb's voice.

"I-Is that Mr. Walker?" From the tone of his voice, the security guard was shocked right down to his big flat feet.

With Caleb reaching for the receiver and Clarence stammering on the other end of the line, she surrendered the phone without another word.

Her worst nightmare had just been realized. Clarence Norton was the biggest gossip in Albuquerque. By the time she and Caleb returned to the office the day after tomorrow, everyone at Skerritt and Crowe would know that they'd spent the night together.

Four

Caleb set the cruise control, then glanced over at the silent woman seated on the passenger side of the truck cab. Other than answering direct questions, Alyssa hadn't said more than a handful of words to him since the kiss they'd shared the night before. She'd been congenial and outgoing enough when she'd discussed financial options and outlined plans for the two potential clients they'd met with in Las Cruces and Truth or Consequences. But whenever they found themselves alone, she clammed up.

"I'm pretty sure we've picked up Mr. Sanchez and Mrs. Bailey as clients," he said, trying once more to draw her out.

She nodded. "It looks that way."

"Are you going to handle their accounts personally or turn them over to someone else?"

"I'll probably turn them over to Richard Henshaw or Marla Davis."

When she let the discussion drop once again, he released a frustrated breath. "Talk to me, Alyssa. Tell me why I'm getting the silent treatment. Is it because of what happened last night?"

Nodding, she stared straight ahead. "I can't stop thinking about Clarence's phone call and the rumors that I'm sure were being passed around the office today."

"You're worried about what's being said at the office?" he asked incredulously. He hadn't given much, if any, thought to the phone call. His mind had been occupied with that kiss. To say she'd damned near knocked his socks off was an understatement.

"Aren't you concerned?" She looked at him like he'd sprouted horns and a tail. "Clarence Norton is the biggest gossip this side of the Mississippi and he's not going to let something like my being in your room at two in the morning go by without putting his spin on it. By now, I'm sure he's told everyone who will listen that we slept together last night."

"Technically, we did sleep together," Caleb said, grinning. "Just not in the same bed." The cab of the truck was dark, but he'd bet every last dime he had that her cheeks had colored a pretty pink. He wished like hell he could see them.

"I suppose that's true. But do you honestly think anyone will believe that?" she asked.

"Maybe." He shrugged. "But the way I see it, our only option is to tell the truth. After we explain things, it'll be up to everyone else to draw their own conclusions."

"You know what that will be." She glared at him like she thought he might be a little simpleminded.

"We can't control what others think or say about us, Alyssa." He gave her what he hoped was an encouraging smile. "But even if they are talking about us now, this time next week someone else will be the topic of conversation around the water cooler."

"I hope you're right."

"I'm sure—"

He stopped short when he noticed steam rolling out from under the truck's hood. Glancing at the temperature gauge on the dash, he said a word that would have had his mother washing his mouth out with soap if she'd heard. It was a dark, moonless night and they were miles away from the last gas station.

"Why is your truck smoking?" she asked, clearly alarmed.

"It's my guess we have radiator problems."

"That's not good." She pushed her owlish glasses up her nose with a brush of her hand—a gesture he'd come to recognize as a sign of her nervousness. "What are you going to do?"

"I'll have to find a place to pull over so I can check

it out." He'd no sooner gotten the words out than they passed a sign indicating a rest area less than a mile ahead. "Looks like we're in luck. At least it will be well lit and I can see what I'm doing."

Ten minutes later, Caleb stood in the parking lot of the rest area with Alyssa peering around his arm at the truck's steaming engine. "The radiator hose is busted," he said when he noticed her questioning expression.

"Do you think you can fix it?"

He shook his head, stepped back and slammed the hood. "I'll have to call roadside assistance." Pulling his cell phone from the clip on his belt, he asked, "Is there another town between here and Socorro?"

She looked anything but happy. "No. This rest area is about halfway between Socorro and Truth or Consequences. And I'm sure that everything in either direction is closed by now."

Pushing the button with the auto club's preprogrammed number, Caleb gave their location and the nature of the problem, then waited for the customer-service representative, identifying himself as Jason, to contact the nearest associate. When the man came back on the line, the news wasn't what Caleb wanted to hear.

"What do you mean they can't get to us until tomorrow morning?" he demanded.

Alyssa cringed. "They won't be here until morning?"

"I'm sorry for the inconvenience, sir. We have only

one associate garage in that area and the mechanic is out on a call," Jason apologized. "After that he has three more to take care of before he can get to you."

Thinking fast, Caleb asked, "Could you send someone with a rental car?"

"Just a moment, please."

"What did he say?" she asked anxiously.

"He's checking." Caleb smiled. "I'm sure we'll have a car here in no time." At least, he hoped they would.

"Sir, your rental car will be delivered to your location by four in the morning," Jason said, sounding as if he'd accomplished something wonderful.

"Four!" Caleb checked his watch, then shook his head. "Five hours is unacceptable, Jason. Even if the car is coming from Albuquerque, it shouldn't take more than a couple of hours."

"I'm sorry, sir," Jason said, beginning to sound like a broken record. "The agencies in both Truth or Consequences and Socorro are closed, the one in Las Cruces has all of its cars rented right now and the one in Albuquerque is having to call someone in to drive the car down to you."

Caleb glanced over at Alyssa. She looked fit to be tied.

"So that's the best you can do?" he asked the young man.

"I'm afraid so, sir," Jason answered. "If there's anything else we can do for you, please let us know."

Caleb snapped the phone shut as he turned to Alyssa.

"I guess you've figured out by now that we aren't going anywhere until around four tomorrow morning."

Looking more pale than she had a few minutes ago, she nodded and started for the passenger door. "I think one of us must be related to Murphy."

"Who the hell's Murphy?"

"I'm not sure, but his law has plagued us throughout this trip."

"Ah, yes. Anything that can go wrong, will go wrong, and at the worst possible moment." He helped her into the truck. "Well, things could be worse."

She looked at him like he had spit for brains. "How on earth could things be any worse?"

He grinned. "We could have broken down before or after we got to the rest area."

"Small consolation," she said, settling herself on the bench seat. "We're still stranded."

"Yes, but at least we're stuck at a rest area with vending machines." He hooked his thumb over his shoulder. "I'm going to see if they have bottled water. Do you want one?"

She nodded. "Thank you."

As Caleb walked the short distance to the row of vending machines, Alyssa took one deep breath, then another. How much anxiety could one woman handle before she lost her mind?

She'd been stressed enough over her behavior when he'd kissed her. Then, after the phone call from the security guard, she'd spent the rest of the night tossing and turning as she'd thought of the office gossip that would surely be spreading like wildfire. Now, she was having to spend another night in Caleb's disturbing presence.

Watching him get bottles of water from the machine, then start back toward the truck, she shivered. He looked darned good in his sports jacket, dress shirt and jeans. On some men, the combination just wouldn't work. But on Caleb, it was sexy beyond words. And she had to admit that spending more time with him wasn't an unpleasant thought. He wasn't just devastatingly handsome, he was intelligent, easy to talk to and had a nice sense of humor. And boy, oh boy, could he kiss.

Her cheeks heated and she had to force herself to breathe. The more time she spent with him, the more she wanted to know about him, the more she wanted him to kiss her again. And therein lay the problem.

For heaven's sake, they worked together. She shouldn't want to spend more time getting to know him. And she definitely shouldn't want his kiss. She knew all too well from past experience that becoming friendly with a coworker spelled disaster with a great big capital *D*.

But the choice had been taken out of her hands. Fate had stepped in and taken over—first with the room mix-up and now with a broken radiator hose.

When he opened the driver's door, he handed her two bottles of water and a package of cookies before removing his sports jacket. Tossing it on the seat between them, he rolled up the sleeves of his white dress shirt, then slid in behind the steering wheel.

Her breath caught and she decided she was in real trouble if all it took to make her insides hum was the sight of his bare forearms. But as he turned up his shirt sleeves, the movement drew attention to the play of muscles and sent her pulse into overdrive.

"I thought you might get hungry while we're waiting on the rental car," he said.

She glanced down at the package of cookies. It was only a stale vending-machine snack, but his thoughtfulness touched her more than she could have imagined. No one, including her father, had ever shown her a lot of consideration. She'd always been the bookish nerd who blended into the background, no matter where she went or who she was with. There had even been times after her mother had died that she'd suspected her father had forgotten she existed.

"Thank you," she said, barely able to get the words past the lump clogging her throat.

"Are you all right?" He reached out to put his arm around her, then, moving his jacket out of the way, pulled her to the middle of the seat. "I know being stuck here is upsetting, but—"

"I'm fine. Really." Wanting to change the subject before she made a complete fool of herself, she asked, "Do you really think going on picnics and getting closer with the employees is going to make Skerritt and Crowe a more efficient consulting firm?"

He nodded. "Let me ask you this. How much do you know about the people who work under you?"

Thinking hard, she shook her head. "Not much."

"Exactly." Twisting in the seat to face her, he leaned back against the driver's door. "Would you say Geena Phillips has been working up to her potential lately?"

She didn't have to think twice about the matter. The woman had been late several times in the past couple of weeks. "No. Lately, she's seemed distracted and I've been meaning to talk to her about it."

"Don't," he said, shaking his head. "A disciplinary talk will only add to the problem."

"I take it you know something I don't."

His mouth flattened into a grim line. "She's battling a case of morning sickness. It's her first pregnancy, she doesn't know where the father of her baby disappeared to and she's scared witless that she won't be able to handle things by herself."

Alyssa was shocked. "I had no idea Geena was going through anything like that."

"That's because in the past it's been company policy to check your private life at the door when you come to work." He shook his head. "Geena's a good accountant who's hit a rough patch in her life. She needs our support and assurance that she's not going to lose the job she'll need to support herself and the baby. That kind of encouragement from an employer can go a long way to instill loyalty in an employee, as well as inspire them to work harder for the company."

She could see where a change was definitely in order in that area. "I'll talk to her about coming in a couple of hours later until she starts feeling better."

Yawning he nodded his approval. "Now you have the right idea." It seemed that he'd no sooner gotten the words out than he was sound asleep.

As she leaned her head back against the seat and tried to get comfortable, she had to admit that Caleb's approach to management made a lot of sense. *By the book* wasn't necessarily the best way to handle employees.

But the idea of letting her employees know her better still made her extremely nervous. The more someone knew about you, the more they could use against you. At least, that was the philosophy her father had preached to her for as long as she could remember.

She sighed. If she stayed at Skerritt and Crowe, becoming friendly with those around her was definitely going to take some getting used to.

Reluctant to open her eyes and end the dream of having two strong arms holding her securely to a wide masculine chest, Alyssa burrowed deeper into her dream lover's embrace. It felt wonderful to be held while she slept and she wanted to enjoy it for as long as she could, even if it was just a dream.

"Good morning."

Her eyes flew open and she started to pull away. Dear heavens, she wasn't dreaming. She was lying on a very real Caleb Walker, who, at the moment, seemed intent on keeping her right where she was.

"I—I'm sorry," she stammered, trying once again to extricate herself from his hold.

He tightened his arms around her and his deep chuckle beneath her ear vibrated all the way to her soul. "Don't be sorry. I'm not. You were comfortable and I thought I'd let you sleep."

Her heart did a funny little flip. "It was nice of you to think of me," she said, straightening her glasses. She managed to put a little space between them to look up into his twinkling hazel eyes. "But—"

"Sweetheart, I think about you more than you realize." He gave her the sexy grin that never failed to curl her toes as he drew her closer, then rested his forehead on hers. "In fact, you're about all I've been able to think of since night before last."

Shivers skittered up and down her spine from the mere memory, but the only way she'd been able to face him had been to tell herself that she'd dreamed it. "Nothing happened," she insisted.

He chuckled. "Then I must have a real vivid imagination, because after that kiss, I walked out of the motel room hotter than a two-dollar pistol at a skid-row pawnshop."

Alyssa felt as if her heart had stopped completely and even if her vocal cords hadn't suddenly become temporarily paralyzed, she couldn't think of a thing to say.

Leaning back, he gazed at her for several long seconds. "You want to know something else?"

"I—I'm not sure," she said, feeling extremely short of breath.

"I want to do it again." He removed her glasses, then placed them on the dash. "Do you want me to kiss you, Alyssa?"

Mesmerized by his remarkable gaze and promising smile, she didn't even hesitate. "Yes."

He removed first one, then another of the pins holding her hair up. "You have beautiful hair. You should wear it down more often."

"I've always hated my hair," she said honestly.

"Why?" Running his fingers through it, he cupped the back of her head and started to draw her forward. "It feels like strands of silk."

Unable to breathe, much less think, Alyssa's eyes drifted shut as she allowed Caleb to nibble at her lips, then cover them with a kiss so tender it made her feel as if she were the most cherished woman on earth. What was there about this man that she couldn't resist?

She'd never had trouble rejecting advances from other men. But when Caleb touched her, rational thought seemed beyond her capabilities. All she wanted was to feel his big, hard body pressed to hers, to taste the desire on his lips and hear his sexy Southern drawl as he said her name.

When he used the tip of his tongue to coax her to open for him, she decided it didn't matter that she had no will of her own where he was concerned. The truth was, she liked the way he made her feel when he kissed her and the last thing she wanted him to do was stop.

As Caleb slipped his tongue inside, Alyssa met him halfway in a sensuous game of advance and retreat and he felt like his heart would pound a hole right through his rib cage. He'd tried to tell himself to leave well enough alone, that Alyssa Jane Merrick was off-limits.

For one thing, she was a career woman and, considering his history with them, he should be running as hard and fast as his legs would carry him in the opposite direction. And for another, he was having to rely on hers and the other managers' experience at Skerritt and Crowe to keep the firm running until he could get some business courses under his belt. He didn't need an emotional involvement added to the mix. It would only complicate things and increase the possibility of one of them getting hurt.

But whether it was wise or not, he hadn't been able to resist the temptation of holding her soft body against his, of once again savoring her perfect lips. He'd spent a hell of a day yesterday and an even worse night reliving that kiss and he needed to know if she was as fantastic as he remembered.

When she lightly stroked his tongue with hers, the sweet, shy response aroused him so fast it made him light-headed and he immediately decided that if anything, his memory had been more than a little faulty. He'd never in all of his thirty years been this turned on by simply kissing a woman.

Slowly tugging her blouse from the waistband of her skirt, he slipped his hand under the beige silk. Her smooth skin felt like satin beneath his palm as he slid it over her ribs to the underside of her breast. Cupping the soft mound, he gently caressed her as he nibbled his way from her lips down the slender column of her throat.

Her tiny moan of pleasure sent a fresh wave of heat straight to his groin. But when he realized that she'd unbuttoned the first few buttons on his shirt and was doing a little exploring of her own, his body tightened with an intensity that quickly had him shifting to relieve the pressure in his suddenly too-tight jeans. Just knowing she was as turned on as he was sent his blood pressure skyrocketing.

At that moment, he wanted her more than he wanted to draw his next breath. He wanted to lay her down and discover all of her secrets. And he wanted to share all of his with her.

"Hey man, get a room."

Glancing through the windshield, Caleb noticed a group of grinning teenage boys walking past the truck on their way to the information center.

Damn! His timing couldn't have been worse. The front seat of his truck in a rest area with God and everybody strolling past wasn't exactly the place for the pleasurable kind of exploring he had in mind.

He took in some much-needed oxygen as he rearranged Alyssa's blouse. "Sweetheart, there's nothing I'd like more than to continue kissing you and a hell of a lot more. But if we keep this up, somebody's going to call the cops. And I'm not real keen on the idea of our being arrested for lewd conduct in a public place."

She made no comment as she stared at him, but the heightened color on her cheeks indicated that she'd forgotten where they were, the same as he had.

"It's daylight," she said, looking around. "What time is it?"

Checking his watch, he shook his head to clear it. "It's a little past eight."

"Where's the rental car?" She slid over to the passenger side of the seat. "I thought it was supposed to be here by four."

Caleb shrugged. "They're late."

"No kidding." She tucked her blouse back into the waistband of her skirt. "Have you called them?"

"The driver thought we were in the rest area north of Socorro," he said, nodding. "When he didn't find us there, he turned around and went back to Albuquerque instead of calling roadside assistance to get a verification on our location."

He didn't add that he wasn't all that sorry the guy was incompetent. Whether it was smart or not, he'd enjoyed holding her while she'd slept.

"Are they sending another car?"

He shook his head. "I told them not to bother."

"You did what?" If looks could kill, he'd be dead in about two seconds flat.

"The mechanic from Truth or Consequences should be here any time with a new radiator hose." He stretched to relieve a few of the kinks in his muscles. "I didn't see the need for a car when he'll have the truck fixed in less than fifteen minutes."

"I suppose that makes sense." She frowned. "But I was hoping we'd be back at the office well before everyone arrived for work. I wanted to run home for a quick shower and to change clothes." She glanced down at her wrinkled suit. "I'm a mess."

"Don't worry about it. We won't get there until midmorning." He gave her his most reassuring smile. "Everyone will be busy and you can get your car without anyone being the wiser."

She looked more than a little doubtful. "I hope you're right."

He didn't tell her, but he hoped like hell he was, too.

Five

When Caleb steered the truck into his reserved parking space, Alyssa immediately noticed that something was wrong with her car. Instead of sitting level, it was tilted to one side. So much for making a quick getaway before someone in the office saw her disheveled appearance.

"Looks like you have a flat tire," Caleb commented when he got out of the truck and came around to open the passenger door for her.

"Great. Just what I wanted to do before I go home," she said, wondering what else could go wrong. "I get to change a tire."

He frowned. "You're going to do it yourself?"

She nodded. "I've been changing my own tires since I learned to drive. My father insisted on it."

"You don't have an auto service plan?"

"No."

He held out his hand. "Give me the keys."

"Thanks, but I'll take care of it," she said, removing her suit jacket.

"Not while I'm around." He took the keys from her, then motioned toward the building. "Why don't you go inside and get out of this heat?"

She nibbled on her lower lip. The temperature was rising, but so was her apprehension that someone would see her.

"I'd rather not."

She could just imagine the stares if she walked into her office looking the way she did. Her clothing couldn't have been more wrinkled from spending the night in the truck and her hair was hanging down her back like a limp mop because Caleb had lost most of the pins when he'd taken it out of her usual chignon.

"Don't be silly." He opened the trunk of her sedan. "It's already in the nineties and—"

"No need for you gettin' all hot and dirty, Caleb," Ernie Clay called as he hurried out of the building toward them. The security guard stopped in front of them, then, grinning like a Cheshire cat, he nodded at her car. "Clarence noticed Ms. Merrick's tire was flat and had me call my brother-in-law. He owns a garage and tow-ing service and should be here in a few minutes to take care of it."

"Thanks, Ernie." Caleb placed his hand at the small of her back and started urging her toward the entrance. "We'll be in our offices. Let us know when your brother-in-law has the tire changed."

The last thing Alyssa wanted to do was walk into the office looking the way she did. But before she had a chance to protest, Caleb ushered her through the building entrance and over to the elevators.

When the elevator door slid shut, she looked down at her clothes. "I'm a complete mess."

He frowned. "You look fine to me."

She shook her head. "My hair is down, my pantyhose has a huge run and I look like a raccoon from the mascara smudges under my eyes."

Removing her glasses for a closer look, he shook his head. "Just one little place under your left eye."

Her jacket fell to the floor as she was thrown off guard by his unexpected touch, and she braced her hands on his chest to keep from falling when the elevator came to a halt on their floor. "I'll take care of—"

The doors opened at that very moment and to Alyssa's horror, Malcolm Fuller and the entire public-relations department observed her clinging to Caleb as he used his thumb to wipe gently at the tender skin below her eye. From the looks on their faces, she could tell exactly what they were thinking.

"Well, hello there," Malcolm said, not even bothering to hide his ear-to-ear grin. "We're headed out to our first team-building picnic. Would you two like to join us?"

"No, thank you," she said before Caleb could get them into something else that would no doubt cause her further humiliation. "But have a good time."

Her cheeks burned with embarrassment as she picked up her jacket, then brushed past the group and headed straight for her office. She didn't wait to see if Caleb followed, nor did she care that he still had her glasses. She'd spent two and a half nerve-racking days with him and she needed some space.

Although her father would strongly disapprove and probably come back to haunt her for being such a coward, all she wanted to do was hide out in her office until her car was fixed. After that, she had every intention of going home, climbing into bed and sleeping the entire weekend. Hopefully, when she woke up Monday morning, she would escape the nightmare she'd been trapped in for the past week.

But even as she mourned the loss of her well-ordered work environment, she couldn't deny that her body still hummed from Caleb's touch. And just the memory of his steamy kisses was enough to leave her aching for things she had no business wanting.

As she walked down the hall toward the conference room to meet with a client, Alyssa finally began to relax.

It had been a week since she and Caleb had returned from the Roswell trip and it appeared that he'd been right about the gossip dying down once they'd told the whole story. To her immense relief, she hadn't heard a single word about them spending the night together or being caught in a compromising position in the elevator. Other than a few smug smiles and knowing looks from a couple of her male coworkers, it had been business as usual around the office.

"Has anyone seen them together since Friday?" Alyssa overheard someone ask as she approached the door to the break room.

The hushed voice stopped her dead in her tracks.

"No. I think they're probably trying to be a little more discreet about their affair." The woman laughed. "I mean really, getting caught in the elevator like that, then trying to convince us that he was looking at her eye. How dumb do they think we are? I heard that half of her clothes were on the elevator floor and she was tearing at his shirt when the doors opened."

A chill raced through her and it felt as if ice water had replaced the blood in her veins. She wanted to scream that they were wrong in their assumptions, that it really was just as Caleb had told them. But she knew it was useless.

"You know there's a door connecting their offices," she heard a third voice chime in. "There's no telling how many times during the day they get together for a little tête-à-tête."

The laughter that followed the erroneous statement made Alyssa nauseous. Feeling as if her world had just caved in on her, she retraced her steps and headed back to her office. She'd heard enough to know that her professional reputation at Skerritt and Crowe had gone down in a blaze of glory—and that there was nothing left but cinders.

"Please call Geena Phillips and have her meet with Mr. Holt in the conference room," she said, placing the client file on Geneva's desk.

"Is something wrong?" the older woman asked, her obvious concern reflected in the tone of her voice. "You don't look like you feel well."

"I don't." That was the understatement of the year, Alyssa thought as she walked into her office and closed the door.

She'd been a naive fool to think that people weren't talking about her and Caleb. How could she have been so stupid? The employees weren't going to discuss their thoughts on the issue in front of the two people involved.

Walking straight to her desk, she sat down at her computer and began drafting her resignation. She'd hoped to have another job lined up before she quit, but the choice had been taken out of her hands. There was no way she could stay at Skerritt and Crowe now. By close of business this afternoon, she'd be unemployed.

"Geneva told me you're sick," Caleb said, walking

into her office without so much as a tap on the connecting door. "Do you need to see a doctor?"

"No." Alyssa should have known their secretary would run to him with her concerns. Geneva, the traitor, had embraced every one of Caleb's ideas and took it upon herself to keep him informed of everything that went on in the office as soon as it happened.

"Are you sure you're all right?" He frowned. "You do look pale. I'll drive you—"

"I'm fine." She glared at him as she keyed in the command to print her resignation. "Now, will you please leave?"

"You don't feel well and you're cranky as hell. But you're fine?" An understanding smile suddenly turned up the corners of his mouth. "That time of month, huh?"

Exasperated, she threw up her hands and sat back in her desk chair. "Why do men automatically think of PMS when a woman wants to be left alone? Did it ever occur to you that I might be tired and just want a little peace and quiet?"

Instead of going back into his office as she requested, he sat down in one of the chairs in front of her desk. "You were on your way to outline a retirement plan that you've been working on for the past week, then all of a sudden you turn the file over to Geena. If you aren't sick, what's the problem?" Before she could answer, he shook his head. "And don't feed me that line about peace and quiet. What's going on?"

Suddenly feeling much too tired to argue, she removed her letter of resignation from the printer, signed it and handed it to him. "I think this is self-explanatory."

He scanned the letter, then shook his head. "You can't resign."

She laughed humorlessly. "I just did."

"I'm not going to accept it." He ripped the paper in half, rose to his feet, then rounded the desk to turn her chair to face him. Placing a hand on each of the chair arms, he had her trapped and she had no alternative but to listen to him. "Talk to me, Alyssa. Tell me what's brought on this sudden decision to bail out of a job I happen to know you love."

His face was only inches from hers and it took every ounce of her concentration to remember what he'd said. "You were wrong," she finally blurted out before she could stop herself.

He frowned. "About what?"

Defeated, she fought to keep her voice even. "The gossip hasn't died down about us. If anything, it's led to more speculation among the employees."

"That's it?"

"Isn't that enough?"

"No."

Caleb's gut churned with a mixture of anger and desperation. He'd known they were still the favorite topic of idle conversation around the office and although he wasn't happy about it, he'd done his best to ignore it. Trying to set the record straight once again would only make matters worse and add more grist to the rumor mill.

Unfortunately, that was only the tip of the iceberg. The possibility of Alyssa leaving the firm was what had him tied in knots. He wasn't proud of having to rely on her without her knowing it, but he needed her expertise to keep things running smoothly until he got a grasp on what he was supposed to be doing.

But as important as her business acumen was to him, the real reason his stomach churned like a cement mixer whenever he thought about her leaving Skerritt and Crowe was far simpler. He'd hated to admit it, even to himself, but he just plain didn't want to face coming to the office without her being there.

Noticing a tear at the corner of her big blue eyes, he removed her glasses and gently wiped it away. "Did you overhear something, sweetheart?"

She nodded. "According to some, you and I are having a grand old time in here." She rolled her eyes. "Several times a day."

He chuckled. "I'm good, but I wasn't aware that I'm *that* good."

Her cheeks turned a pretty pink. "I wouldn't know anything about that. But I do know that I can't effectively supervise when everyone thinks I'm sleeping with the boss."

Lifting her chin with his index finger, he stared at her for several long seconds. God, she was pretty and it tore him up to see her upset like this.

"It's going to be all right, Alyssa. I promise."

"I don't know how."

She looked so dejected, it was all he could do to keep from taking her into his arms. But that would only add fuel to the fire if someone walked into her office and caught them.

As he continued to stare at her, a germ of an idea began to form. It was crazy enough that it just might work.

"I think I have a solution that will stop the tongues from wagging and allow you to keep your job here," he said, smiling.

She looked doubtful. "I'm listening."

"Let's go along with the rumors."

He laughed when she looked at him like he might not be playing with a full deck. "Have you lost your mind?"

"Probably." He took her hands in his, then pulling her to her feet, took her in his arms. "My grandpa used to say that sometimes the only way to put out a fire is to throw kerosene on it."

"In other words, insanity runs in your family?"

Caleb grinned. "Grandpa did have his share of peculiarities, but most of the time his logic made a hell of a lot of sense. Toss a little fuel on a fire and it burns itself out real quick and that's the end of it. Leave it alone and it can smolder for a while, then flare up again and again."

"Would you care to explain how that relates to our current problem?" To his satisfaction, she'd wrapped her arms around his waist and seemed genuinely interested in hearing him out.

"If we come out in the open and tell everyone that we are romantically involved, there won't be anything left to speculate about." He paused as something else came to mind. "In fact, as of right now, we're engaged. Then, in a few weeks, we'll announce that we've changed our minds and decided to just be friends."

"Now I'm sure you've gone over the edge." Pulling away from him, she stepped back and shook her head. "It would never work."

"Sure it will. And the sooner we announce our big news the sooner we'll be back to business as usual." Giving her a quick kiss, he reached over to press the button on her intercom. He wasn't waiting for her to come up with any more arguments why his plan was faulty. "Geneva, call a mandatory meeting of all employees for two this afternoon in the lobby downstairs."

"Consider it done," the secretary answered. "Is there anything else?"

"Nope. That's it. Thanks, Geneva." Turning back to Alyssa, he smiled. She had that deer-in-the-headlights look again. "Relax. In about an hour, we'll make our big announcement and the problem will be over."

She sank into her chair as if her knees would no longer support her. "Or just beginning."

"Trust me, sweetheart. An engagement is just what the doctor ordered to take care of this little problem."

She sighed. "Which doctor would that be? Kevorkian?"

Laughing, he headed back into his office. "Hang on to your sense of humor and everything will work out great. You'll see."

When he closed the door behind him, Caleb walked over to stare out the window behind his desk. A fake engagement? What the hell had he been thinking?

But when Alyssa had shoved her resignation at him, he'd felt like his stomach had dropped to his shoe tops. And it hadn't been entirely due to the fact that he needed her to stay at the firm and keep things running while he took his classes.

The simple fact of the matter was he didn't want Alyssa to leave because he had a case of the hots for her and there didn't seem to be any way he could stop it. Not even reminding himself of his miserable track record with a career woman had lessened her appeal. Since their trip to Roswell last week, all he'd been able to think about was how soft and sweet she'd looked when she slept and how good it had felt to hold her.

He took a deep breath and shook his head in an effort to clear it. If they were going to convince the Skerritt and Crowe employees they were wild about each other, it was going to take some planning.

A slow grin spread across his face. They had an entire weekend to get their act together and he knew the perfect place to hold their strategy session. Now all he had to do was convince Alyssa to go with him.

* * *

"This is never going to work, Caleb," Alyssa said as they walked out of her office into the deserted hall.

"Just follow my lead and act happier than you've ever been in your life." He waited for her to step onto the elevator. "I'll take care of the rest. Did you get your purse?"

She nodded. "Although I can't understand why you think I need it."

"You'll see."

His grin told her that he had something up his sleeve, but she didn't have time to think about what it could be. What was about to take place was foremost in her thoughts and had her wondering if they'd both lost their minds. In just a few short seconds, the elevator doors were going to open and they'd tell the entire Skerritt and Crowe staff they were engaged.

When the elevator came to a halt on the ground floor, Caleb grinned and took her hand in his. "Ready?"

"No."

"Smile," he whispered as the doors swished open.

Stepping off the elevator, instead of looking deliriously happy, she'd bet everything she owned that she looked more like she was about to throw up. The sick feeling intensified when she watched several of her colleagues exchange knowing glances.

"Since our trip to Roswell last week, there's been a lot of speculation about the nature of the relationship between me and A.J.," Caleb said, getting right to the heart of the matter. "That's why we've called you all here this afternoon. We want to end the speculation and set the record straight, once and for all."

There was no turning back now. She took a deep breath and trained her unwavering gaze on Caleb. She wasn't certain she'd be able to get through the next few minutes if she had to look at anyone else.

"Yes, there's something going on between me and A. J. Merrick." Her heart skipped several beats when he looked down at her and smiled. "I'd like to announce that as of this afternoon, Alyssa and I are engaged."

Stunned silence reigned for several seconds before the crowd suddenly broke out in a round of enthusiastic applause. But when Caleb pulled her to him and kissed her like a soldier returning from war, the cheers were so loud it was almost deafening.

When he raised his head, he announced, "Alyssa and I are leaving town for the weekend, so don't try calling us. We'll be busy making..." His pause and suggestive grin caused several knowing smiles. "Wedding plans," he finished. He pointed to Malcolm. "You're in charge until we return on Monday."

The kiss and Caleb's announcement that they were going away together had taken her by surprise, but he shocked her beyond words when he swept her up into his arms and carried her from the building to the uproarious cheers and applause of the Skerritt and Crowe employees. Unable to find her voice and not knowing what else to do, she threw her arms around his shoulders and hung on for dear life.

"What in the name…of all that's holy…do you think you're doing?" she finally managed to squeak out as he walked across the parking lot toward his truck.

He laughed. "I'm whisking you away like any white knight worth his weight in beans would do when he's won the hand of his fair maiden."

"Don't you think you're taking this farce just a bit far?" she asked when he opened his truck door and deposited her on the bench seat.

When she started to scoot over to the passenger side, he slid behind the steering wheel and pulled her up against him. "If this is going to work, we have to look like we're wild about each other, right?"

"Yes, but—"

"Don't you think everyone would expect us to spend time together away from the office?" he asked, starting the truck, then backing it from the parking space. "And especially right after we got engaged?"

She sighed. "All right, you've made your point."

He gave her a grin that curled her toes inside her black pumps. "We'll drop by your apartment for you to get some clothes together, then head up to my place to hide out for the weekend."

Feeling as if her life was spinning out of control with no hope of recovery, she gasped. "I beg your pardon.

When did this fiasco escalate to me actually going away with you?"

As he drove the truck out onto the street and headed in the direction of her apartment, he shook his head. "Think about it, Alyssa. Ed Bentley lives in the same complex you do. In fact, he and his wife live in the building across the street from yours. Even if you stayed in for the entire weekend, he'd notice your lights going on and off and know you were home." He gave her a pointed look. "The success of our plan hinges on this, sweetheart."

Her temples began to throb and her stomach felt as if it had been filled with rocks. "Why did I ever let you talk me into this?"

"Because the rumors and gossip were getting to you." He took her hand in his to give it a gentle squeeze. "Besides, we need to map out a game plan for how we'll play our engagement and eventual breakup."

Everything he said made perfect sense, but that did little to lessen the apprehension building inside her as he steered the truck into her apartment complex. She didn't even have a clue where he lived.

As if he'd read her mind, he smiled. "Be sure to bring a jacket. It gets chilly at night."

"You live in the mountains?" Somehow, she wasn't surprised.

"Yep. About twenty miles from here, in the East Mountain area," he said, parking in front of her building. He shrugged. "I never have been much of a city boy."

She took a deep breath and reached for the door handle. "I'll pack accordingly." When he started to get out of the truck, she shook her head. "If you don't mind, I'd like a few minutes alone to collect my thoughts."

He stared at her for a moment before he nodded. "Don't forget to pack your swimsuit. I have a hot tub and pool."

As she entered her small apartment to begin packing a few things for her weekend away with Caleb, Alyssa wasn't sure whether to laugh or cry. Why on earth had she allowed him to talk her into such a ridiculous scheme?

But as she finished folding clothes into her small bag, then made arrangements with Mrs. Rogers to take care of her parakeet, Alyssa knew exactly why she'd gone along with Caleb's plan. She simply didn't want to leave Skerritt and Crowe to find a position elsewhere. Other financial firms might offer the same opportunities to do the work she loved, but there was one thing they didn't have—a handsome CEO with hazel eyes, a sexy as sin grin and kisses that turned her into melted butter.

Six

Opening the wrought-iron gate, Caleb wondered what was going through Alyssa's pretty little head as he led her across the courtyard to the front door. The farther out of the city they'd driven, the more silent and speculative she'd become.

"If you're worried about the sleeping arrangements, don't," he said when they entered the house. He set her small case down to punch the deactivation code into the security system. "There are three extra bedrooms. You can take your pick."

"I really hadn't given where I'd be sleeping much thought." When he turned to face her, she gave him a sheepish grin. "I've been mentally calculating how much stucco homes cost and what the investment potential in real estate is on this side of the Sandia Mountains. I would think that the equity would build quickly since this area seems to be growing pretty fast."

He chuckled as he picked up her overnight case. "Once an accountant, always an accountant, huh?"

"Something like that." She gave him an odd look. "With your background in business, wasn't it something you considered when you moved here?"

"Not really." He wasn't about to tell her that the house had been given to him when he'd accepted Emerald's offer to take over the firm or that his background in business started two weeks ago when he'd walked through Skerritt and Crowe's front doors. "I was more interested in the fact that it's fairly secluded and has several acres of land."

She seemed to accept his explanation and, breathing a little easier, he followed her into the great room. But his heart damned near hammered a hole clean through his rib cage when she stopped to stare at a portrait of a middle-aged Emerald Larson and her infamous playboy son, Owen—Caleb's late father.

"Are they your relatives?" she asked, smiling.

The picture was at least twenty-five years old and it was apparent that Alyssa hadn't recognized the pair. Hopefully, she wouldn't.

"That's my grandmother and father," he said cautiously.

Gazing at him a moment, she nodded. "There's a strong family resemblance."

He placed his hand at the small of her back to usher her toward the bedrooms before she had a chance to study the picture closer and figure out who they all were. He hadn't lied to her thus far and he wasn't about to start now. If she'd recognized the Larsons, he'd have admitted to being one of the heirs to the Emerald, Inc. conglomerate. But she hadn't. And although omission of the facts was something he wasn't proud of and continued to struggle with, being outright dishonest was out of the question. It just wasn't his style.

"Feel free to check out the other two bedrooms, then decide which one you want," he said, opening the door to the room closest to his. The room had been done in yellow and green and looked a little more feminine than the other two bedrooms. "They all have their own private bathroom, but this one is the only one besides the master suite that has a sitting area."

"This is fine," she said, glancing around. She walked over to the French doors on the opposite side of the room to look out at the patio and pool. "It's a lovely area and your home is beautiful, Caleb. You must love living up here."

"Thanks." He set her bag on the end of the bed, then walked over to stand behind her. "The terrain is a lot different here than in Tennessee, but I'm getting used to it." He didn't tell her that it was a far cry from the humble farmhouse he'd grown up in or that he was having a hard time thinking of it as his, even though it had been signed over to him when he'd accepted Emerald's offer.

"I'd like to hear about where you used to live," she said, sounding wistful. "I've never been east of the Mississippi, but I've heard the southern states are quite beautiful."

"They are. Back home when I look at the mountains, I'm used to seeing them covered with trees, and everything is green. Here it's just as pretty, but in a different way. There aren't as many trees and everything is shades of tan, brown or orange." Without thinking, he slipped his arms around her waist and drew her back against him. "I'll have to take you to see the eastern mountains sometime."

He heard her soft intake of breath a moment before she turned to face him. "Caleb, what are we doing?"

Staring down at her, he wondered the same thing. She was the type of woman he'd vowed to steer clear of, yet there was something about Alyssa Jane Merrick that he couldn't resist. He wanted to show her where he'd grown up, wanted her to know who he was and what had molded him into the man he'd become, and he wanted to know all about her. And that scared the living hell out of him.

Suddenly needing to put a little space between them in order to figure out what the hell had gotten into him, he kissed her forehead then, releasing her, started for the door. "While you get your things put away and freshen up, I'll go see what I can scare up for supper."

As Alyssa watched him leave the room, she sighed

heavily. It hadn't been lost on her that he'd avoided answering her question. Could he be as confused about what was going on between them as she was? What *was* happening between them?

She certainly wasn't an expert at affairs of the heart, but it was evident there was something drawing them together. They couldn't be in the same room for longer than five minutes without being in each other's arms.

What was there about Caleb Walker that made her forget the lesson she'd learned five years ago at the hands of a man just like him? Hadn't she suffered enough humiliation when she'd learned that men weren't above using women to achieve their own goals or advance their careers?

Sitting on the side of the bed, she thought about Wesley Pennington III, the man who'd taught her just how cutthroat the business world could truly be and the lengths that some men were willing to go to in order to get ahead. Handsome and charming, Wesley had swept her off her feet about a year after they'd both started working at the prestigious financial group of Carson, Gottlieb and Howell. And right up until the end of their six-week affair, she hadn't had a clue that he'd been using her to gain information about a potential client.

But as she mentally compared Caleb to Wesley the weasel, she had to admit there were very few, if any, similarities. Wesley wouldn't have been caught dead in a pair of jeans and boots, nor would he have chosen to live in a secluded house in a quiet rural area over his ultramodern uptown condo. And that was just scratching the surface of how the two men differed.

Wesley had been a polished sophisticate and tended to act superiorly with anyone below him on the corporate ladder. But Caleb wasn't anything like that. His casual, down-to-earth personality immediately put everyone at ease and he not only treated those who worked for him as his equals, he seemed to genuinely care about them as well.

That was something she knew firsthand to be beyond Wesley's capabilities. He didn't care about anyone but himself and he wasn't above stepping on those who posed a threat to, or got in the way of, his lofty ambitions. He hadn't thought twice about using her affections for him to gain information that had led to his obtaining a coveted corporate account and ultimately the promotion that rightly should have been hers. When she'd confronted him about it, he'd readily admitted that he'd only started dating her for the purpose of getting ahead. But the most devastating blow had come when she'd overheard her coworkers gossiping about the whole sordid mess. That's when she'd decided she had no alternative but to look for another job and had found her present position at Skerritt and Crowe.

But she was certain Caleb would never stoop to that level, would never take credit for her or anyone else's accomplishments, even if he wasn't already the head of

Skerritt and Crowe. Nor would he publicly humiliate her. On the contrary. He'd come up with the pretend engagement and had her spending the weekend with him because he was trying to squelch the rumors and gossip that she found hurtful.

Sighing, she put the last of her clothes in the dresser drawer, then changed into a pair of baggy camp shorts and a T-shirt. She'd tried every way in the world not to like Caleb. But the truth of the matter was, she trusted him more than she had anyone in a very long time. And whether it was smart or not, she might as well admit it—if she hadn't already fallen for him, she was well on her way.

"Thank you for a delicious dinner. You're a very good cook."

"Not really." Caleb grinned. "Throwing something on the grill and fire roasting a few vegetables is about the only thing I know how to fix, besides frying bacon and scrambling eggs."

"Well, I thought it was scrumptious." Her sweet smile did a real number on his insides. "And I'm glad you suggested we eat out here on the patio." He watched her look past the pool at the valley below. "The view is absolutely gorgeous."

He couldn't agree more; the view was beautiful. But he wasn't looking at the cedar trees or the valley. The woman seated at the table with him was far prettier than anything he'd ever seen.

Rising to his feet before he did something stupid like take her in his arms and kiss her senseless, he gathered their plates. "I like sitting out here after the sun goes down. Other than an occasional coyote howling, it's pretty quiet."

"Let me help with those," she said, standing up.

He shook his head. "I'll take care of the cleanup."

"That's not fair," she protested. "You cooked. I should clear the table."

He started toward the house with the dishes. "While I'm doing this, why don't you change? I don't know about you, but I could use some time in the hot tub before I turn in for the night."

"That does sound wonderful, but are you sure I can't help you first?"

Damned if she didn't follow him into the kitchen. Taking a deep breath, he shook his head. He was about two seconds away from kissing her until they both needed CPR or carrying her to his bedroom to make love to her for the rest of the night. But he couldn't tell her that. She'd probably belt him a good one, then run as hard and fast as she could back to Albuquerque.

"I'll just put these plates in the dishwasher, then meet you in the hot tub in ten minutes," he said, surprised that his voice sounded fairly steady. Considering his state of mind and the changes his body was going through at that very moment, he figured it was nothing short of a miracle he could talk at all.

"Okay." She gave him a smile that caused his blood

pressure to shoot up a good fifty points. "But I'm cooking breakfast tomorrow morning."

"You've got yourself a deal, sweetheart." He'd agree to just about anything as long as she left the room and let him get a grip on his runaway libido.

But as he watched her walk away, his heart stalled and his body tightened so fast it left him feeling lightheaded. Even though her khaki shorts and pink T-shirt looked to be a couple of sizes too big, it couldn't disguise the sexy sway of her shapely hips or the fact that her long, slender legs looked like they could wrap around a man and take him to heaven.

Caleb closed his eyes and forced himself to breathe. What the hell had he been thinking when he'd suggested they get in the hot tub? If just watching her walk made him hard, what would happen when he saw her in a swimsuit?

The mental image his overactive imagination conjured up made his knees wobble and sweat pop out on his forehead and upper lip. Leaning against the kitchen counter for support, he groaned. How on God's green earth was he going to keep his hands to himself for the next two days?

When the phone rang, he was grateful to whoever was on the other end of the line for interrupting his disturbing thoughts. "Thank you."

"You're welcome. Now, do you want to tell me what I did?"

"Hey, Hunter." Once he and his brothers had learned

about each other, they'd all, by unspoken agreement, stayed in touch. And Caleb was happy with the bond they were forming.

"What's up with answering the phone the way you did?"

"Just thinking out loud," Caleb said, hoping his oldest brother forgot about his slip of the tongue.

"How's the financial world? Any new advice on how I can turn my savings account into a fortune?"

"If you want to build your money, the best advice I can give you at this point is to leave it where it's at," Caleb said dryly.

Hunter snorted. "You sound about as sure of yourself at this financial stuff as I feel about running an air-ambulance service."

Caleb smiled. "How's the EMT course going?"

There was a pause before Hunter finally answered. "I've been in that damned class for almost two weeks and I still get light-headed whenever I see a needle."

"At least you've stopped passing out at the sight of them," Caleb said, laughing.

"Just barely." Obviously wanting to change the subject, Hunter asked, "Are you going to attend Emerald's birthday party at the end of the month?"

It was Caleb's turn to snort. "I don't think we've been given a lot of choice about going. The invitation read more like a summons than a request to help her celebrate her seventy-sixth birthday."

"It sounds like the one I got." Hunter laughed humorlessly. "I knew that old gal was going to yank our chains every chance she got."

"Have you talked to Nick lately?" Caleb asked.

"He called me last night and suggested we all meet for a beer before we attend Emerald's party."

"That's a good idea." Caleb chuckled. "Maybe if we have a buzz going, it'll make the evening more tolerable."

"I like the way you think."

Finalizing plans to meet before the party, Caleb hung up and headed for his bedroom to change. He was looking forward to seeing Nick and Hunter again. And his only regret about finding out that he had two brothers was that he hadn't learned of their existence sooner.

But he really had no room to complain. He'd had a great childhood with the love and guidance of his maternal grandparents and a mother who had been totally devoted to raising him the right way. He'd asked who his father was a few times, but his mother would only smile and tell him to be patient—that one day he'd learn all about the man. After a while he'd given up asking, and if he'd missed having a father, Caleb couldn't ever remember it. His grandfather had taught him everything he'd needed to know, from how to tie a fishing lure to what it meant to be a good, honest man.

But as he pulled on a pair of gym shorts, he decided he couldn't say he'd missed knowing his manipulative paternal grandmother. No matter what she said about not meddling in their lives back then or the way they ran the businesses she'd given them now, he had a feeling she still had their every move under surveillance and would have no problem stepping in to take over if she felt it was warranted.

But when Caleb opened the French doors to step out onto the patio and spotted Alyssa standing by the hot tub, his grievances with Emerald Larson were quickly forgotten. Damn, but Alyssa looked good. Her black one-piece bathing suit clung to her body and enhanced all the curves that he'd been fantasizing about ever since walking into her office the day he'd arrived to take over the financial firm.

He swallowed hard. He'd been right about her legs, too. They were long, sleek and perfect for holding a man close while he made love to her.

"I'm sorry." Walking over to her, he had to clear his suddenly dry throat. "It took longer than I planned. One of my brothers called."

"I heard the phone ring." She smiled wistfully. "It must be nice to have siblings."

"You're an only child?" He wasn't ready to tell her that a little less than a month ago, he hadn't even known his brothers existed.

Nodding, she took off her glasses and, laying them on a nearby chair, started to climb the steps to get into the hot tub. "I always wanted a brother or sister to share memories with, but it wasn't meant to be."

Caleb took hold of her arm to help steady her as she stepped into the bubbling water, but the second his fingers touched her satiny skin, a jolt of electric current zinged straight up his arm and exploded in the pit of his belly. Climbing into the hot tub on shaky legs, he sat down beside her and tried to think of what they'd been talking about.

"I, uh, haven't always been close with my two brothers."

"Is there a big age difference between you?" she asked, sounding genuinely interested.

"No, we're all about the same age." He knew he was walking a fine line, but he wanted to be as truthful with her as possible. "We had the same father, but different mothers." Deciding it was time to change the subject before he revealed more than he intended, he smiled. "Could you tell me something, Alyssa?"

"It depends on the question and whether or not I know the answer," she said, looking a little apprehensive.

"Why do you go by your initials at work, instead of your given name?" He'd wanted to know the answer since reviewing her personnel file. "It's very pretty." *Like you.*

She shrugged one slender shoulder. "That's what my father always called me. I think it was his way of pretending I was the son he always wanted, but never had."

Reaching out, Caleb traced his index finger along her porcelain cheek. No matter what kind of hell he'd have to go through, he couldn't seem to stop touching her. "I'm sure he loves you more than you realize, sweetheart."

She remained silent for several long moments before nodding. "I suppose it was possible that he cared for me, but it's something I'll never know. He died on a mission in the Middle East during my junior year in college."

Caleb felt like a complete jerk for bringing up an obviously painful subject. Without thinking twice, he lifted her onto his lap and did his best to ignore how her shapely bottom felt pressed to his rapidly hardening body.

She stared at him for several long seconds. "Caleb, this isn't a good idea."

"Hush." Cradling her to his chest, he held her close as the water bubbled around them. He tried to tell himself that he was offering her comfort, but the truth was she felt so right in his arms, he couldn't bring himself to let her go. "I'm sorry, Alyssa. I didn't mean to pry."

"It's all right." He felt her begin to relax against him. "I've never had any illusions about it. My father and I didn't have a great relationship."

He kissed her temple. "What about your mom? Are you close to her?"

"Mother passed away when I was eight." She sighed. "That's when I started attending school at the Marsden Academy for Girls."

"Your dad sent you to a boarding school?" Anger burned at his gut. How could Merrick have done that to his only child? Caleb could only imagine how lonely and scared she must have been. At that moment, he despised the man for abandoning her when she'd obviously needed him most.

"Actually, Dad didn't have a lot of choice about sending me to Marsden," she said softly. "He was a navy SEAL and never knew when his team would be called out on a mission."

"Couldn't you have stayed with a relative?"

He wondered why her grandparents hadn't stepped forward to take her in. There was no way in hell his grandparents would have ever turned their grandchild away. They'd stood by his mother when she'd found herself pregnant and alone, and had helped her raise him, even though it hadn't been as socially acceptable then as it was now for a single woman to have a child.

Alyssa shook her head. "I've never even met my grandparents. My dad was raised in the foster-care system and my maternal grandparents didn't think he was good enough for their only child. When my mom eloped with him on graduation night, her parents more or less disowned her."

Alyssa had no idea why she was telling Caleb about her family or, more accurately, her lack of one. Normally, she didn't share any details about herself with anyone. But he was easy to talk to and his compassion made her feel at ease and free to discuss it for the first time in years.

"What about you?" she asked, enjoying the feel of

his wide bare chest against her arm. "What was your childhood like?"

"It was pretty average," he said, shrugging. "I grew up on a farm in central Tennessee—"

"If you hadn't told me before that you were from the South, I'd have never known," she said dryly.

He chuckled. "You can take the boy out of the South, but you can't take the Southern accent out of the boy."

"Something like that," she said, laughing. Wanting to hear more about his childhood, she asked, "What was it like growing up on a farm?"

"I guess it was pretty much like growing up anywhere else," he said, thoughtfully. "I did most of the things other kids my age did—played Little League baseball, helped Grandpa around the farm and went skinny-dipping in the creek every chance I got." His mischievous grin curled her toes. "Still do."

Her insides fluttered. "You swim in the nude?"

He nodded. "I don't even own a pair of swim trunks. The only reason I'm wearing gym shorts now is to protect your tender sensibilities."

She suddenly felt a warmth course through her that had nothing to do with being in the hot tub. "I've never gone swimming without a suit."

His grin caused her to feel as if the water temperature rose a good ten degrees. "You should give it a try sometime."

She'd never been good at sexy banter and, unable to

think of a suitable comeback, she asked, "Where did you go to school?"

His muscles tensed slightly before he answered. "No private academies for me. I went to public schools."

"University, too?"

"There's no other team like the University of Tennessee Vols."

"Vols?"

"Short for Volunteers," he said, smiling. He pulled her closer. "But I don't want to discuss schools or sports teams right now." He brushed his lips over hers as he slid his finger under one of the straps of her swimsuit. "Do you have any idea how great you look in this little black number?"

She'd purposely ignored the fact that she was still sitting on his lap, but suddenly several things became quite apparent. They were alone in the semidarkness; their water-slick bodies were pressed together and his muscular thighs under her bottom weren't the only things that were hard.

Her eyes widened and a breathtaking charge of need filled every cell in her being. "I think…I'll move over to the seat."

"I like you right where you are." With one arm around her waist, he held her in place as he slid his hand from her shoulder down her upper arm, taking her swimsuit strap with him. "Your skin feels like silk, Alyssa."

Desire so hot she felt scorched by its intensity washed over her and, closing her eyes, she sighed. "This is insanity."

"Do you want me to stop?" he asked, his voice so low and intimate it caused goose bumps to shimmer over her skin.

God help her, but she didn't want him to stop. She wanted him to kiss and hold her. She wanted to feel his strong hands caressing her body. And if she was really honest with herself, that's what she'd wanted since their trip to Roswell.

She shook her head as she opened her eyes to meet his questioning gaze. "That's what's insane. I don't want you to stop. I should. But I don't. And that's what's so confusing. I've never been the type of person to throw caution to the wind." A shiver streaked up her spine when he cupped her cheek with his palm and she had to take in some much-needed air before she could finish. "But being with you, I find that I don't want to analyze every move I make. I don't want to be sensible. And living for the moment suddenly sounds so very tempting."

"It's up to you, Alyssa. All you have to do is tell me what you want and I promise to respect your wishes." He smiled. "But if it's left up to me, I'll take this suit off of you and show you just what temptation is all about."

His sexy drawl made her insides hum and all of her

secret places pulse with a hunger stronger than anything she'd ever experienced. "I want you to make me feel alive. I want you to touch me and..." She took a deep breath. "More."

Seven

As he gazed at her, Caleb wondered if he'd lost every ounce of sense he'd ever possessed. He had an incredibly desirable woman sitting on his lap, telling him that she wanted him. And what he was about to say could very well end things before they ever got started.

But his sense of honor wouldn't allow him to proceed without giving her the chance to call a halt to it right here and now. He had a feeling it was going to be one of the most meaningful nights of his life and he didn't want her regretting one minute of what they would share.

"Alyssa, I'm going to tell you something and I want you to think about it very carefully."

She looked apprehensive. "Okay."

He took a deep breath and went on before he had a chance to change his mind. "If I continue, I'm not going to stop. I'm going to take this bathing suit off and kiss every inch of your beautiful body. I'm going to touch you in places that will make you moan with pleasure. I'm going to do things to you that will drive you crazy and have you calling my name when you find your release. And then, when you think I'm finished, I'm going to start all over again."

To his immense relief, instead of the small spark of desire in her luminous blue eyes dimming, it grew to a hunger that matched his own. But he needed to hear her say the words, needed for her to tell him that she wanted him to make love to her.

"Is that what you want, Alyssa?"

"Yes." There wasn't a moment's hesitation in her simple answer, nor a hint of reservations in her steady gaze.

Groaning, Caleb covered her mouth with his, then traced her perfect lips with his tongue. If she'd told him no, he'd have had a hell of a time finding the strength to walk away. But she hadn't. And just knowing she wanted him enough to let down her guard made him hot in ways he'd never imagined.

Her contented sigh encouraged him and he took advantage of her acceptance to slip inside and once again explore her sweetness. As he tasted and coaxed her with strokes that mimicked a more intimate union, he decided that kissing Alyssa was quickly becoming as addictive to him as any drug.

The way she held on to him, the way she responded to his kiss was all any man could dream of and proved what he'd thought from the moment they'd met. She wasn't the emotionless woman she tried to lead her coworkers to believe. She was warm, affectionate and, if her enthusiastic response to his kiss was any indication, passionate as hell when she let herself go. He just thanked the good Lord above that he was going to be the man holding her when that happened.

As he worshipped her with his mouth, he moved his hands over her shoulders and down her arms to slide the top of her swimsuit out of the way. He wanted to feel her soft body melting into the hard contours of his. But when he pulled her more fully against him, nothing could have prepared him for the reality of having her firm breasts pressing into his chest, their pebbled nipples scoring his skin.

"You feel so damned good," he rasped as he kissed his way from her mouth to the tender skin just below her ear.

Shuddering against him, she whispered close to his ear, "Please…don't stop."

Turning her to face him, he lifted her until her breasts cleared the surface of the warm water. "Sweetheart, there's not a chance in hell of that happening."

Slowly moving his lips over her creamy skin, he made his way from her shoulder down the slope of her breast to the hardened tip. Taking the tight bud into his mouth, Caleb sipped the water droplets from her puckered flesh, savored the sweetness that was uniquely Alyssa.

As he sucked and teased her nipples, a moan of pleasure escaped her parted lips and, raising his head, he asked, “Does that feel good?”

“Mmm.” Threading her fingers through his hair, she held him close. “It’s wonderful.”

Suddenly needing to feel all of her against him, Caleb quickly shoved her swimsuit down her hips and legs, then tossed the wet black spandex over the side of the hot tub. His gym shorts quickly followed.

Reaching for her, he pulled her to him and the feel of smooth female skin against his hair-roughened flesh sent a flash fire to every nerve in his being. He wanted to take things slowly, to do all the things he’d promised, but his body was urging him to stake his claim and make her his.

“Alyssa, I want you so damned bad I can taste it,” he said through gritted teeth. “I think we’d better get out of here and—”

“Please, Caleb,” she said, wrapping her arms around his shoulders. Her eyes were glazed with hungry need when she added, “I need you inside. Now.”

At her throaty plea, a shaft of longing rushed through him at the speed of light and white-hot desire enveloped him. With his mind clouded to anything but the need to possess her, he sank to his knees and lifted her to him.

Determined to enter her slowly, he clenched his back teeth together so hard it would probably require surgery to separate them. But as he guided himself to her, she proved his other theory about her when she wrapped her long, slender legs around his waist and her body consumed his in one smooth motion. He definitely felt like he was in heaven.

But her quiet gasp, the tightness surrounding him, penetrated the haze of passion. If he'd caused her any discomfort at all, he'd never forgive himself.

"Did I hurt you? You're really tight, sweetheart."

"It's been a…while." She nibbled at his neck and damned near caused him to have a coronary when she whispered, "You feel absolutely wonderful right where you are."

Crushing her coral lips beneath his, he kissed her until they both gasped for breath. "I'm so hot right now…" He closed his eyes in an attempt to slow down. "I think I might just spontaneously combust."

She touched his cheek with one wet finger as she moved her lower body. "Make love to me, Caleb."

Her request and the motion of her body unleashed the hungry need he'd been trying to hold in check and, groaning, he began to thrust into her. He'd never had a woman hold his body quite so perfectly or respond to him in ways that, until tonight, he'd only imagined in his wildest fantasies.

But as ideal as the moment was, the warm water bubbling around them enhanced the spirals of fiery passion binding them together and he could feel her body straining for the same mind-shattering release that he'd been trying to forestall from the moment they'd become one. All too soon her feminine inner muscles held him captive, then quivered as he felt the tight coil inside her let go. The sound of her whispering his name and the amazing sensation of her pleasure triggered his own release from the tension gripping him. Groaning, he thrust into her one final time and held her to him as he emptied himself deep inside of her.

With their energy completely spent, they clung together for several long moments before reality began to clear his passion-fogged brain. Saying a word that he usually reserved for smashed thumbs and drivers who cut him off in traffic, he eased away from her.

"What's wrong?" she asked, clearly alarmed by his harsh curse.

He ran an unsteady hand across the tension gathering at the back of his neck. "Tell me you're on the pill or patch or some kind of birth control."

"N-no. It hasn't been an issue for several years." As she stared at him, her eyes suddenly grew wide. "We didn't—"

He shook his head. "I'm sorry. There's no excuse for me not taking precautions."

She nibbled on her lower lip for a moment. "I probably don't have anything to worry about."

"We," he said, placing his hands on her shoulders. "I want you to know that we're in this together, Alyssa. If you do become pregnant, I'll be right there with you every step of the way."

"I'm tired," she said suddenly. "I think I'll take a shower and turn in."

Caleb didn't try to stop her when she climbed out of the water, wrapped herself in one of the towels and, grabbing her glasses, hurriedly disappeared through the doors into her room. They both needed time to come to terms with what they'd shared and the possible consequences of his carelessness.

He couldn't believe he'd been so thoughtless. Where the hell had his mind been, anyway?

In the past, he'd never failed to use protection. Even before knowing who his irresponsible father was, Caleb had been determined not to be anything like the man who had impregnated Caleb's mother, then left her to face things on her own. He'd always made it a point never to get so carried away that he lost sight of what an unexpected pregnancy could mean for him or his partner.

But he'd been so turned on, so mind-numbingly hot for Alyssa, the thought of protection hadn't even crossed his mind. All he'd been able to think about was how perfectly she fit within his arms, how soft her body was and how her sweet kisses warmed him to the depths of his soul. His body hardened at the very thought of how amazing their lovemaking had been and had him wanting nothing more than to go inside and make love to her for the rest of the night.

Cursing a blue streak, he splashed out of the hot tub and made a beeline for the pool. When he dove into the much cooler water and started swimming laps, his muscles protested, but he didn't care. He had to get himself under control.

When he reached the end of the pool on his tenth lap, he stopped to catch his breath and, glancing toward the French doors, shook his head. His body still throbbed with a need that left him dizzy and he had a feeling he could swim from now until his dying day and not even come close to easing the burning ache to make Alyssa his once again.

Climbing out of the pool, he wrapped a towel around his waist and, picking up his gym shorts and her swimsuit, headed for his room. He had a feeling one of two things was going to happen this weekend. Either they were going to make love again or, first thing Monday morning, he was going to be seeking medical attention for a perpetual erection.

Alyssa stared at the ceiling as she thought about what had happened in the hot tub. She still couldn't believe what had taken place when Caleb had touched her, nor did she understand it. It was as if she'd been taken over by a shamelessly uninhibited wanton who not only lived for the moment, but threw caution to the wind and didn't even consider the possibility of the consequences.

She'd never in all of her twenty-six years acted that way before. Not even when she and Wesley had been seeing each other and she'd thought she was in love had she experienced a total loss of control. And that scared her as little else could.

But all it took was one kiss, one touch of Caleb's hands and she lost all sense of herself. It was as if she became part of something larger than either of them, emotionally as well as physically. If his reaction was any indication, he'd experienced it, too.

The best thing she could do for her own well-being and peace of mind would be to have him take her back to Albuquerque tonight. Then, first thing Monday morning, insist that he accept her resignation, effective immediately.

She knew their coworkers would question why their "engagement" was off and why she no longer worked at Skerritt and Crowe. But that couldn't be helped. Caleb could tell them whatever he liked about the matter. She wouldn't be there to hear their comments and speculation on what might have happened between them.

Tossing the sheet aside, she climbed out of bed and pulled on her robe. The sooner she got back to the safety of her apartment, the better. Not only could she finish updating her résumé, she needed to check her personal calendar. Until she did that, she really wasn't certain whether she needed to worry about an unplanned pregnancy.

"Caleb?" She tapped on his bedroom door. "Are you still awake?"

When there was no response, she turned to go back to her room. She'd only gone a couple of steps when the door opened.

"Did you need something?"

The sight of him standing in the doorway in nothing but a pair of white cotton briefs rendered her temporarily speechless and all she could do was nod.

When they'd gotten into the hot tub there hadn't been enough daylight left to see the details of his body, then, when he'd removed his gym shorts, they'd been in the water. But the light from his bedside lamp cast just enough light now to enhance the ridges and ripples of his well-defined muscles and drew attention to the fact that Caleb Walker was perfection and then some.

His heavily padded pectoral muscles, bulging biceps and sculpted shoulders were proof that he'd spent years doing a lot more on that farm than just going skinny-dipping. Her gaze drifted lower and her pulse sped up.

Caleb's stomach had so many ripples it resembled a washboard. But it was everything below the waistband of his white briefs that had her gulping for air. The stretchy cotton hugged him like a second skin and outlined the size and heaviness of his sex. The lack of a tan line on his long, muscular legs was confirmation that he did, in fact, swim in the nude.

"You look a little shook up."

Why wouldn't she be? He was standing there practically naked and didn't seem the least bit self-conscious about it.

Taking a step toward her, he placed his hand on her shoulder. "Are you all right?"

Nodding, she tried to remember why she'd knocked on his door, but the feel of his warm palm touching her through her thin robe made it extremely difficult to breathe, let alone think.

He stared at her for several long seconds before he smiled and lightly touched her cheek with his index finger. "We need to talk, sweetheart."

Her insides fluttered wildly and she couldn't seem to catch her breath. "I…agree. I have something I need to ask you."

He stepped back and motioned toward his open door. "Let's go into my room and sit down."

She shook her head. "I'm not sure that's a good idea."

"I think it is." Before she could stop him, he grabbed her hand and tugged her into his bedroom. "I have something I need to do."

"Caleb—"

"It's all right, Alyssa." Leading her past the bed to the sitting area by the French doors, he sank into one of the armchairs, then pulled her onto his lap. "I want you to listen to me before you say anything. Will you do that?"

"Y-yes."

Why was she allowing him to take command of the situation? Why wasn't she demanding that he immediately take her back to Albuquerque before something else happened? But with all of the bare male skin surrounding her, she found she was too distracted to do much of anything but go along with what he wanted.

"Good." He gently stroked her hair as his hazel gaze held hers captive. "I want to apologize for the way I acted earlier and set the record straight. I wasn't upset with you, Alyssa. I was mad as hell at myself for letting you down. I know that's no excuse. But the truth of the matter is, I failed you, then acted like a real bastard about it. And I'm sorry, sweetheart."

Her conscience wouldn't let him shoulder all of the responsibility. "You weren't in that hot tub alone. I'm just as much to blame as you. I should have thought—"

He stubbornly shook his head. "It's a man's place to protect a woman."

"I beg to differ. Both partners should share the responsibilities of prevention." When he looked like he was going to protest, she reached up to place her finger to his lips. "But I'm not going to argue that with you now. I think it's safe to say we both got a bit carried away."

"You're right about that, sweetheart." His sexy grin sent waves of heat coursing through her. "I was so hot for you, I'm surprised we didn't cause the water in the hot tub to boil."

His candor and the sound of his low drawl caused her to feel as if the blood in her veins had been replaced with warm honey. Deciding it would definitely be in her best interest to move before she lost sight of what she needed to ask him, she started to stand up.

"Hey, where are you going?" he asked, holding her in place. He brushed his lips over hers in the gentlest of kisses. When he raised his head, he asked, "Didn't you say you had something you wanted to ask me?"

With every cell in her body tingling and her heart skipping every other beat, how was she supposed to think? Why had she knocked on his door? For the life of her, she couldn't remember.

But Caleb didn't seem to mind that she had temporary amnesia. Giving her a promising smile, he lowered his head again to kiss her with such tenderness it brought tears to her eyes. As he used his tongue to trace her lips, spirals of desire slowly swirled to every part of her and a shiver of excitement skipped up her spine. All he had to do was touch her and her will to resist melted away like mist under an early summer sun.

As he teased her to open for him, then dipped his tongue inside to explore her inner recesses, she was shocked at her own eager response. Boldly stroking him, she wrapped her arms around his shoulders and pressed closer.

His groan of pleasure rumbled up from deep in his chest and the vibration against her breasts sent a flash of heat streaking through her at the speed of light. When he broke the kiss, his lips seared a path from her neck to her collarbone, making her feel as if she were about to go up in flames.

He pushed her gown and robe aside to continue a blazing trail of nibbling kisses to the valley between her breasts and Alyssa was certain she'd been branded by the intensity of it. The ribbons of need flowing through her began to wind their way to the pit of her stomach, forming a coil of hungry desire deep in the most feminine part of her.

Seated on his lap, she knew immediately when his body began to change, to grow hard with the same passion that was overtaking her. Right or wrong, wise or not, she wanted to be warmed by the heat of his desire, to once again have him claim her body and soul.

"Please, Caleb."

"I want you again, sweetheart." His drawl sounded rough and impassioned. He raised his head to give her a look that seared her all the way to her soul. "Do you remember what I told you in the hot tub?"

"I—I'm not sure." She was about to burn to a cinder and he wanted her to recall something he'd said earlier?

The wicked grin he gave her sent a wave of goose bumps shimmering across her skin. "I promised you that I was going to kiss you all over. That I was going to touch you in all of your secret places and make you cry out with pleasure. Then, when you think I'm finished, I'm going to start all over again."

His suggestive words caused the coil in her stomach to tightened to an empty ache that robbed her of breath.

"And I have every intention of keeping that promise." His intense hazel gaze made her feel as if she'd melt right then and there when he added, "I'm going to love you the way you deserve to be loved. Right here. Right now."

Alyssa's pulse pounded in her ears and without a moment's hesitation, she nodded that she wanted that, too.

It fleetingly crossed her mind that she was playing with fire and there was a very real possibility that she'd end up being burned. But she didn't want to think about that now. She wanted to be held and touched and loved by the man who had stolen her heart.

Eight

If Caleb had given her time, Alyssa might have panicked at the realization that she'd fallen in love with him. But he was already taking matters into his own hands. Lifting her as if she weighed nothing at all, he stood up with her in his arms and walked over to his king-size bed.

Setting her on her feet, he held her gaze with his as he slowly untied her robe and slid it from her shoulders. "This time we're going to take things slow and easy. I want to savor every inch of you and by the time I'm through, there won't be a doubt in your mind about how special I think you are."

With every word he spoke, her limbs felt a bit weaker

and the restlessness deep inside her grew stronger. "I'm going to hold you to that," she said, wondering if that sultry female voice was really hers.

He slid his palms along her arms, then, taking her hands in his, he lifted them to kiss each one of her fingertips before placing them on his shoulders. "I'd rather you hold *me* to you."

She threaded her fingers through the hair at his nape, then, drawing his head down for her kiss, she pressed herself to his hard frame. "There are a few things that I want to do to you, too. Holding you against me is just one of them."

If she'd thought about it, she might have been appalled at her shamelessness. But it was as if she shed every one of her inhibitions when Caleb took her in his arms. And, for the first time in her life, she felt free to explore her own sexuality.

His smile increased the humming in the very core of her as he gathered her nightgown in his hands and slowly pulled it up over her head. "Let's get the rest of these clothes off."

Tossing the peacock-blue silk to join her robe on the floor, he ran his hands along her sides to her hips, then, hooking his thumbs in the elastic waistband of her panties, slowly pushed them over her hips and down her thighs. Once she kicked them aside, he stepped back to strip himself of his briefs. Her breath caught and an ache of pure need filled her at the sight of him.

She'd been right. Caleb's body was sheer perfection. Hard and lean, there wasn't a spare ounce of flesh anywhere on him.

But it was the sight of his strong arousal that caused her heart to skid to a stop, then take off at a gallop. He was above average in height and it appeared that other things about him were above average as well. If she hadn't already experienced the power of his lovemaking, she might have been a bit apprehensive. But she trusted Caleb implicitly. Although he'd been as excited for her as she'd been for him, he'd taken great care not to hurt her when they'd made love in the hot tub.

"You're beautiful." His voice was so reverent, so filled with awe that she had no doubt that he meant what he said.

"I was thinking the same thing about you," she said softly. "You're perfect."

As he took a step toward her, his deep chuckle made her feel as if the temperature in the room had suddenly risen several degrees. "I'm not perfect, sweetheart, but you know what they say about practice."

She felt color flood her cheeks. "I didn't mean—"

"I know. But I intend to spend the rest of the night making sure our lovemaking is perfect for *you,*" he said, reaching for her.

If his words hadn't sent her into total meltdown, the feel of his hard male flesh against her softer female skin would have. A shudder ran through his big body and she knew he felt the same scorching heat she did.

Closing her eyes, she reveled in the differences between a man and woman—the contrast of hard ridges to soft curves. "I love the way your body feels pressed to mine."

As he lowered his head, his slow grin held a wealth of promise. "I like the way I feel inside you more."

Her knees wobbled and, feeling as if she'd melt into a puddle at his feet, she sagged against him. Opening her eyes to gaze up at him, she whispered, "I do, too."

Without warning, he swung her up into his arms, placed her in the middle of his bed, then stretched out beside her and pulled her to him. "Keep talking like that, sweetheart, and I'll go off like a Roman candle on the Fourth of July."

Before she could respond, he captured her lips with a desperate hunger that sent a flash fire streaking all the way to her soul. But when he broke the kiss to nibble his way from her collarbone down the slope of her breast, then took the tight bud into his mouth, she felt as if she'd burn to a crisp. His gentle sucking, the feel of his tongue on her sensitized nipple caused the spiraling heat to increase the tension building deep in her womb.

A moan escaped as she held his head to her. The delicious sensations Caleb created with his erotic teasing were driving her absolutely wild.

"Do you like that?" he asked, kissing her abdomen.

Nodding, she shivered from the exquisite feeling of his warm breath whispering over her. "Please…"

He dipped his tongue in the indention of her navel as he ran his calloused hands along her sides. "Tell me what you want, Alyssa."

"M-more."

"Are you sure?"

There was an underlying tone, a warning of sorts in his quiet question. He was asking for her trust, asking for permission to take her places that no man had taken her before.

"Yes!" If he didn't do something soon she was going to die from wanting.

Without another word, he raised his head and the blazing passion she saw in his hazel eyes stole her breath. Sliding his hands over her hips, then down her legs, he held her captive with his heated gaze as he caressed the insides of her thighs. Her heart pounded hard beneath her breast as inch by slow inch he came closer to the nest of curls at the apex of her thighs. When he finally reached his goal, pleasure radiated throughout her body at his featherlight touch.

"Oh, my!"

"Does that feel good?" he asked as he continued to drive her mad.

"Yes."

"More?" His deep drawl was as seductive as the feel of his hands on her.

"P-please!"

His kiss on the inside of her thigh sent a tingling excitement straight to her core. Clenching her eyes shut, she gripped the sheet with both hands. "I feel like…I'm on fire."

"Easy, sweetheart. It's only going to get better." He'd no sooner gotten the words out than he lowered his head and gave her the most intimate kiss a man can give to a woman.

Shock waves of pure ecstasy raced through her and she couldn't stop a moan from escaping. "C-Caleb, please…I need—"

Kissing his way back up her body, he nibbled at one of her aching nipples. "What do you need, sweetheart?"

"You. Now."

"Why?" he asked, treating the other taut nub to the same sweet torture.

"I can't…take…much more."

"Open your eyes, Alyssa." When she did as he commanded, he shook his head. "Remember what I told you?"

"N-no." He expected her to think at a time like this?

His promising grin sent another wave of heat flowing through her veins. "I told you that just when you think I'm finished, I'm going to start all over again."

If she could have found her voice, she'd have told him that much more and she'd go stark-raving mad. But before she had the chance, he lowered his head and held true to his promise.

Worshipping her body with his hands and lips, Caleb took her to the crest again and again. But just when she thought she'd find the peace of sweet release, he'd pause just long enough for the tightening inside her to ease a bit, then he'd start all over again.

"I can't take…another second…of this." The tension inside her was so great that it made her feel as if she were coming apart at the seams. "Please…make love to me, Caleb. N-now."

His kiss was so tender it brought tears to her eyes. "Just a minute, sweetheart." He slid open the bedside table to remove a foil packet. "I'm not going to let you down a second time," he said, rolling the condom into place.

With their protection arranged, he took her into his arms, then, nudging her knees apart, held her gaze with his as he moved to cover her. Her pulse thundered in her ears as he slowly, carefully sank himself deep inside her welcoming body.

When he was completely immersed within her, she watched him close his eyes and she knew he was fighting for control. "I think…I've died…and gone to heaven," he said, the strain of his struggle evident in his husky voice.

Tilting her hips, she felt him sink into her a fraction more. "Take me to heaven with you, Caleb," she whispered close to his ear.

His big body shuddered and a groan rumbled up from deep in his chest a moment before he opened his eyes to stare down at her. The hungry need in the hazel depths matched her own and as he eased himself back, then forward, she wrapped her arms around him and joined him in the wondrous dance of love.

Holding her gaze with his, he set a slow pace that tightened the pit of her stomach and made her feel cherished in a way she'd only dreamed of. He must have realized the delicious sensations within her were building to a crescendo because he strengthened his thrusts and Alyssa found herself straining to reach the summit.

She was suddenly there and, as the coil inside her burst free, she cried out his name as she shattered into a million shards of brilliant light. Tightening her arms around him, she tried to absorb him into her very soul as she rode the waves of utter and complete fulfillment. No more than a second later, she felt Caleb tense, then heard him call her name as he found his own release from the storm.

When he collapsed on top of her, she held him close as her heart filled with an emotion like nothing she'd ever felt before. She'd done her best to resist. But in that moment, she knew beyond a shadow of doubt that she'd done the unthinkable. She'd fallen in love with Caleb Walker.

The following Friday afternoon, Caleb sat at his desk tapping his ink pen on the polished surface as he stared off into space. As far as work went, he hadn't been worth a damn all week. All he'd done was sit around with a sappy grin on his face and think about how fantastic the past weekend had been and how totally amazing Alyssa was.

Her response to his touch had been everything a man could ever dream of, and he'd been just as hot for her. They'd spent the entire time making love, falling asleep in each other's arms, then awakening to make love again.

When his lower body tightened, he took a deep breath and willed himself to relax. All he had to do was think about her and he got aroused so fast it made him dizzy.

But his desire to be with her wasn't just physical. Once he'd gotten to know the real woman behind those baggy suits and owlish glasses, he'd found that she was warm, compassionate and had a great sense of humor.

He grunted. How on God's green earth had he ever thought her to be anything like Leslie Ann?

Even if he hadn't checked the personnel records and found her employee evaluations, he would have figured out that Alyssa had used her brains and education to get where she was with Skerritt and Crowe. She'd worked her cute little tail off and hadn't had to step on anyone's toes to get the promotion to operations manager six months ago.

But Leslie Ann had taken the easy way to the top. She'd done anything and everything to climb the corporate ladder. Hell, he could even remember a couple of times when she'd bragged about taking credit for the hard work of those working under her. And her barracuda instincts hadn't stopped there. He had no doubt that she'd have crawled off her deathbed just for the chance to attend a party where she could schmooze with the big boys. Nor was she above kissing a few executive rear ends along the way to get what she wanted.

Disgusted with himself for wasting two years chasing after such a selfish, self-absorbed woman, he shook his head. Leslie Ann had never been, nor would she ever be half the woman Alyssa was. And somewhere between walking into her office that first day and sitting here thinking about their weekend together now, he'd fallen for her.

His heart stalled and he felt like he couldn't breathe. When had Alyssa gotten past his defenses? Why hadn't he seen it coming?

He sat for several long minutes feeling as though he'd just been run over by the Tennessee Titans' entire defensive line. His timing couldn't have been worse. He'd barely taken over running Skerritt and Crowe and he hadn't attended one of his classes at the university, let alone earned a degree.

Propping his elbows on the desk, he buried his head in his hands. Now that he'd found Alyssa, he wasn't about to let her go. But what could he do about the situation? There was no way in hell they could build a relationship unless he came clean and told her who he was and that he didn't have anything more going for him than a high-school education.

He raised his head to stare blindly out the plate-glass window at downtown Albuquerque. He'd boxed himself into one hell of a corner.

How was he going to tell her that he was a fraud, that he wasn't really qualified to run a financial consulting firm? And how would she react when she found out that he was one of Emerald's grandsons?

"Caleb, you have a call on line one." Geneva's voice coming through the intercom broke into his unsettling thoughts.

He depressed the talk button. "Take a message, Geneva."

"It's Mrs. Larson," Geneva said, as if in awe of Emerald.

Great. Just what he needed right now—a conversation with his manipulative grandmother. "Thanks, Geneva. I'll take the call."

Taking a deep breath, he picked up the phone. "Hello, Emerald."

"Caleb, darling, how are you?" Emerald Larson might be at least three-quarters of a century old, but she looked and sounded like a much younger woman.

"I'm tied up with something pretty important right now." At the moment, his newly discovered feelings for Alyssa and trying to figure out what he was going to do about them took top priority. "Could I call you back this evening?"

"Of course. You have the number at the mansion, don't you?"

"It's on speed dial at the house."

"Good. I retire around ten," she added. "I'll expect your call before that."

Before he could say another word, she hung up. "Well, goodbye to you, too," he muttered, replacing the receiver.

He briefly wondered what Emerald wanted, but he quickly dismissed the call when Geneva's voice once again came across the intercom. "Caleb, you're needed in the break room."

"Can't it wait?"

When Geneva failed to answer, he impatiently walked over to open the door to the outer office. The secretary was nowhere in sight.

"Did you just get a page from Geneva to go to the break room?" Alyssa asked, walking out of her office.

He nodded. "Did she tell you what was going on?"

"No." She looked around the deserted office. "Where is everyone?"

Shrugging, he walked over to take her in his arms. "Beats me."

As he gazed down at her, he didn't think he'd ever seen her look more beautiful. Since their weekend together, she'd started wearing her hair down and she'd replaced her baggy dark suits with pastel silk blouses and linen slacks. Today she wore pink and tan and looked so damned lovable she took his breath away.

"Have I told you how incredible you look today?" he asked, kissing the tip of her nose.

Her breathless laughter sent a shaft of longing straight to the region below his belt buckle. "I was thinking the same thing about you."

"We need to talk," he said suddenly. He wasn't sure how she'd react when he told her everything about himself and the reason he'd taken over the firm, but he knew for certain there couldn't be any secrets between them. "Come home with me for the weekend."

"I'm not sure—"

"I am," he said, nodding. "Remember, we're supposed to be planning our wedding. Don't you think we'd be expected to spend our weekends doing just that?"

"My poor parakeet will think I've abandoned him," she said, laying her head against his chest.

He wasn't about to let a bird keep him from being with the most desirable woman he'd ever known. "We'll take him with us."

"Are we going to discuss my ideas for the break room?"

"Among other things," he said, distracted by the feel of her softness.

"There you are," Geneva called from down the hall. She looked extremely flustered. "Please hurry. We need you both in the break room. It's an emergency."

"What's wrong, Geneva?" With Alyssa hot on his heels, Caleb jogged down the hall. But when he entered the room, he stopped dead in his tracks. "What the hell?"

"What's going on?" Alyssa asked, bumping into his back.

"Congratulations!" the entire Skerritt and Crowe staff shouted in unison.

Shocked to see all of the firm's employees crammed into the break room, it took a moment for Caleb to figure out what was going on. He and Alyssa were the guests of honor at a surprise engagement party.

"Oh, my dear heavens." Alyssa's cheeks colored a deep rose and her baby-blue eyes were round with disbelief.

"We wanted you two to know how happy we are for you," Geneva said, dabbing at her eyes with a lacy handkerchief.

Caleb put his arm around Alyssa's shoulders to draw her to his side. "I think I speak for both of us when I say we really didn't expect you all to do this."

"I...we truly don't know what to say," Alyssa added, leaning against him as if her knees were about to buckle.

"Well, I do." Grinning from ear to ear, Malcolm Fuller stepped forward and handed them each a champagne flute. "Since I'm the oldest employee here at Skerritt and Crowe, I have the honor of being the first to toast the happy couple." Clearing his throat, he held his own glass high. "It's with great pleasure that I have the opportunity to celebrate Caleb and Alyssa's happiness. May your engagement be brief and your wedding perfect, and your honeymoon go on for a lifetime." His voice grew gruff. "Congratulations, kids. You make a beautiful couple."

As they listened to several others express their good wishes, Caleb realized that was exactly what he wanted—a long and happy life with Alyssa at his side. He wanted to make love with her every night and wake up with her in his arms each morning for the rest of his life.

When she glanced up and smiled at him, he knew he'd walk through hellfire and back just to make her happy. And if she'd let him, he had every intention of making their pretend engagement real.

Nine

After a leisurely swim, Alyssa sat between Caleb's legs on a lounge chair by the pool, watching the shadows of evening fade into the dark of night. What were they going to do now? she wondered. The surprise party had been a wonderful gesture and she really appreciated their coworkers' thoughtfulness, but it had also greatly compounded an already complicated situation.

She and Caleb couldn't break off their "engagement" right away. It would look far too suspicious and without a doubt, everyone would know that it had been a sham from the beginning.

Unfortunately, continuing their pretend commitment posed an even bigger problem for her. The more time she spent playing the role of Caleb's loving fiancée, the more she found herself wishing their engagement was real.

"You're mighty silent tonight, sweetheart." Caleb's whispered drawl caused a wave of goose bumps to shimmy over her skin as he pulled her back against him to wrap his arms around her.

She sighed. She wasn't about to tell him the real reason for her pensive mood. "I like watching the shadows cover the valley as the sun goes down."

His low chuckle seemed to vibrate right through her. "Besides the scenery, is there anything else you like about being here?"

"Hmm, I really like the pool," she teased.

He nuzzled the side of her neck. "Anything else?"

She closed her eyes as a wave of need swept over her. "The hot tub…is very…nice."

"Yes, it is," he murmured against her skin. "It's very relaxing." He nibbled her earlobe. "It's really wet." He nipped her shoulder. "It's definitely hot." Slipping the top of her swimsuit down, he covered her bare breasts with his warm palms as he kissed her temple. "And it's a great place to make love."

Her heart thumped her ribs and her breathing grew shallow. "If I remember correctly, that's what you said about the pool, your bed, the sofa in the great room, the—"

He nodded. "Anywhere is a good place to make love with you, sweetheart."

"We proved that last weekend." With his hands caressing her breasts and his growing arousal pressed to her bottom, Alyssa felt as if her insides had been turned to warm pudding. Closing her eyes as her temperature rose, she added, "I think we made love in every room in the house, as well as out here by the pool and in the hot tub."

Shaking his head, he chafed her nipples with the pads of his thumbs. "There's one place we haven't made love." He kissed the nape of her neck, then set her away from him. Rising from the lounge chair, he held out his hand. "And I think it's high time we changed that, don't you?"

Without so much as a moment's hesitation, she placed her hand in his and let him pull her to her feet. As they walked through the French doors to his bedroom, she reminded herself that she should resist temptation, run as hard as she could back to her apartment and protect what was left of her heart.

But when he led her into the master bathroom and turned her to face him, she realized that she didn't have a choice in the matter. Staring up into his intense hazel eyes, she knew it was far too late to save herself. Her heart was no longer her own. It belonged to Caleb, and it had from the moment he'd swaggered into her office the day he'd arrived to take over Skerritt and Crowe.

Smiling, he peeled her damp swimsuit away, then tossed it aside. "Your body is way too beautiful to cover up with clothes."

She grinned. “Even at work?”

As he lightly slid his hands from the swell of her breasts down to her hips, the wicked gleam in his eyes stole her breath. “I don’t share. Seeing you this way is for my eyes only, sweetheart.”

“That street goes both ways,” she said, tugging his wet gym shorts from his lean hips. “I love the way your body looks, too. But I wouldn’t want any other women appreciating it the way I do.”

He took her into his arms as he lowered his head. “Only for you, Alyssa. Only you.”

He fused his mouth with hers then, and the promise in his gentle kiss, the feel of his muscular body surrounding hers caused her pulse to race and stars to dance behind her closed eyes. The warmth of need that she only experienced in Caleb’s arms flowed through her—heating her blood, filling her with passion so strong it made her weak in the knees.

His arms tightened around her as he slipped his tongue inside to entice her with the taste of his hunger, and a fluttering swirl of desire began to form in the very core of her. But when he ran his hands down her back to cup her bottom and lift her closer, the feel of his hard arousal pressed to her lower belly caused an answering tightness deep within her and a delicious ache to commence in all of her feminine places.

Lost in the sensations he'd created inside her, she vaguely realized that he was moving them into the large tiled shower, closing the door and turning on the water. He tightened his arms around her once again to pull her to him and the feel of his wet skin against hers sent ribbons of excitement twining to the most interesting places.

Sliding his hands along her sides, then back up to cup the heaviness he'd created in her breasts, he lowered his head to sip the trickling water from her aching nipples. He teased first one hardened tip, then the other and by the time he raised his head to kiss her, she tingled all over.

Caleb's gaze held her spellbound as he reached for the soap, then ran it over her shoulders, her breasts and down her abdomen. His slick hands touched her everywhere, sliding over her skin, sending tiny sparks of electricity skipping over every nerve in her body and it took all of her concentration just to remember to breathe.

Determined to treat him to the same sensual massage, she smiled as she took the soap from him. Lathering her trembling hands, she smoothed them over his wide chest, rippling stomach and lean flanks. She wanted to give to him as he'd given to her and, taking him in her palms, she slid her fingers along his taut skin, measured his length and the strength of his need for her.

He closed his eyes and a deep groan of pleasure escaped his parted lips. "Sweetheart, if I die right now, I'll leave this world a happy man."

"But I don't want you to be just happy," she said, wondering if she had the nerve to take her exploration to the next level. "Open your eyes, Caleb." When he did as she commanded, she waited until the water had rinsed away the last traces of soap. "I want you to be fulfilled."

Caleb's heart stalled and he didn't think he'd ever breathe again as he watched Alyssa sink to her knees in front of him. "Sweetheart, you don't have to—"

At the feel of her sweet lips on his heated body, he stopped abruptly and clenched his teeth together so hard he'd probably end up with a broken jaw. Her intimate kiss was sending liquid fire streaking though his veins at the speed of light and he wasn't altogether sure how much longer his legs were going to support him.

Placing his hands on her shoulders, he lifted her to her feet. "If you keep that up much longer, fulfillment won't be an issue."

She smiled. "You don't like what I was doing?"

"I didn't say that." He drew some much-needed air into his lungs and shook his head. "The problem is, I like it too much. But I want both of us to be there for the grand finale. And I fully intend to be inside you when that happens."

He lowered his head to swirl his tongue around one beaded nipple, while he chafed the other one with his thumb. Teasing her with his teeth, then sucking the tight tip into his mouth, he slid his hand down between them to find the sensitive nub at the apex of her thighs. She trembled against him as he gently stroked her and he decided that he'd like nothing better than to spend the rest of his life bringing her pleasure.

By the time he raised his head to gaze at her beautiful face, her porcelain cheeks were painted with the rosy glow of passion and her baby-blue eyes sparkled with deep longing. Her heightened excitement fueled his own and Caleb suddenly needed to possess her body and soul.

"Do you want me, Alyssa?"

"Yes."

"Now?"

"Yes."

Somehow he found the strength to step back and momentarily leave the shower. When he returned with their protection in place, he turned her away from him, then wrapped his arms around her and pulled her back against his chest.

"Caleb?" Her uncertainty was evident in the tone of her voice.

"Do you trust me, Alyssa?" When she nodded, he kissed her shoulder. "I'm going to caress your body while I make love to you."

He supported her weight as he lifted her to him and in one smooth motion entered her from behind. Her soft moan of pleasure mingling with his deep groan sent waves of hot, urgent desire coursing from the top of his head all the way to the soles of his feet and he had to struggle to retain what little control he had left.

The feel of her holding him deep inside, her inner muscles clinging to him as she adjusted to his size almost sent him over the edge. But, determined to ensure her pleasure above his own, he covered her breasts with his hands then, kissing her shoulder and the slender column of her neck, slowly began to rock against her.

Their water-slick bodies moving in perfect unison caused the pulse in his ears to roar and, wanting her to find the same release that was rapidly overtaking him, he slid his hand down to touch her intimately. Stroking her with a rhythm that matched the movement of their bodies, he felt her inner muscles constrict, then gently caress him as she found the culmination they both sought. Her release triggered his own and, holding her to him, he shuddered as he followed her over the edge and gave up his essence to the woman he loved.

When his mind began to clear, Caleb carefully lowered Alyssa to the tiled floor, then turned her to face him. Even with her hair hanging wet and limp around her shoulders, she was the most beautiful woman he'd ever had the privilege to lay eyes on and he had every intention of making her his—permanently.

But he couldn't do that until he'd told her everything—who he was, why he'd been sent to run the financial firm and that he lacked the credentials to do the job right. He just hoped liked hell she'd forgive him for not telling her about himself from the beginning.

"We need to talk, sweetheart."

Wrapping her arms around his waist, she grinned. "Here?"

He smiled as he shook his head. Standing buck naked in the shower wasn't exactly the best place for the kind of confessions he'd be making. "Let's dry off and get in bed."

"I like the sound of that."

Taking her by the hand, he pulled her out of the shower. "I'm going to make sure you like doing it even more."

The next morning, when Alyssa woke to the sound of Caleb warbling an off-key version of a popular country song, she couldn't keep from smiling. She found his habit of singing while he showered quite endearing. But in the few short weeks they'd known each other, she'd come to realize there wasn't anything about him that she didn't find completely irresistible.

He was outgoing and compassionate and when they made love, he never failed to ensure her pleasure before finding his own. And even though she'd had serious doubts about him taking over Skerritt and Crowe, she had to admit he was an absolute genius in his approach to management. Since his arrival, employee morale had been greatly improved, productivity was on the rise and they'd signed several new clients.

But as she lay there thinking about all the reasons she'd fallen in love with him, she couldn't help but wonder what he wanted to discuss with her. He'd mentioned before the party, then again in the shower last night that they needed to talk. But when they'd toweled each other dry, their insatiable hunger had taken over and, after making love again, they'd immediately fallen asleep.

Had he decided their role-playing posed too great a threat to his peace of mind? Was he wanting to discuss how they were going to handle breaking off their pretend engagement?

Her stomach clenched painfully at the thought of never being held in his strong arms, of never tasting his need for her in his tender kiss. She'd given her heart to him, but she had no idea how he felt about her.

Deciding that she had a few questions of her own that needed to be answered, she tossed the covers aside and got out of bed. She grabbed his shirt from one of the chairs and quickly pulled it on. Sleeping with him in the nude was wonderful, but they needed to talk without being distracted again.

She got halfway across the room, but the ringing phone stopped her. Glancing at the clock, she wondered who on earth would be calling this early on a Saturday morning. She frowned when she read the words *No Data* on the caller ID.

As she stood there wondering if she should let the machine pick up the call, Caleb stopped singing. "Could you get that, Alyssa?"

"Sure." She picked up on the third ring. "Hello?"

There was a moment of silence, then a commanding female voice demanded, "Who am I speaking with?"

Alyssa frowned at the censure in the older woman's voice. "Who are you wanting?"

"My grandson, Caleb Walker. Is he there?"

"He's unavailable at the moment. Could I take a message?"

"Is this Ms. Merrick?" the woman asked, suddenly sounding much more pleasant.

"Yes, it is." How on earth had the woman known who she was?

"Emerald Larson here. I thought I recognized your voice. How have you been? I don't think we've had a chance to talk since I called to let you know Caleb would be taking over the firm."

Alyssa felt as if her stomach had dropped to her feet. Emerald Larson, one of the most successful businesswomen ever and the first female to break into the Fortune 500 top ten, was Caleb's grandmother?

"I must thank you for everything you've done for Caleb, my dear. I've heard the two of you make a great team," the woman went on. "Considering Caleb's lack of education, making the transition from simple country farm boy to running a financial firm the size of Skerritt and Crowe was a major challenge. But I'm not surprised that he's been successful. He has the Larson genes, after all."

"Of course," Alyssa said, feeling more sick inside than she'd ever felt in her life.

"I'm sure that once he gets a few college courses

under his belt, he won't have to rely so heavily on you to run things. But rest assured, my dear, I'll see that you're well compensated for your efforts."

Alyssa had to get off the phone before her fragile composure shattered into a million pieces. She'd done it again. She'd fallen for a man who only wanted to use her to accomplish his goal. The only difference this time was that she'd fallen hopelessly in love with Caleb.

"I really need to go, Mrs. Larson. I'll tell Caleb to call you."

Before the woman could respond, Alyssa broke the connection. When she looked up, Caleb was walking through the bathroom door as he secured a towel around his waist.

"Who was that?"

"Your grandmother." Walking over to place the cordless phone in his hand, she fought to keep her voice even as she looked into his incredible hazel eyes. "Emerald Larson. She wants you to call her."

When he reached for her, Alyssa successfully sidestepped his touch. "Please, don't."

His expression stoic, he took a step toward her. "Let me explain, Alyssa."

"I think your grandmother explained things quite clearly. You've been using me to keep the firm running while you played at being the successful businessman." A sudden rush of emotion threatened to choke her and she had to take a deep breath before she could finish.

"You know, I never paid much attention to the tabloid headlines about Owen Larson and his nefarious escapades." She laughed humorlessly. "I should have. Maybe I'd have recognized the same traits in his son and avoided making a fool of myself."

"Alyssa—"

Shaking her head, she impatiently wiped a tear from her cheek. "I can only imagine how pathetically desperate for a man I must have appeared to you. The frumpy numbers cruncher whose entire life revolved around her job." Straightening her shoulders, she drew on a lifetime of being taught to face the enemy with courage and grace. "But that no longer matters. Please tell your grandmother that I don't want, nor do I need, the compensation she mentioned."

His scowl deepened. "Compensation?"

"I'm certain she was unaware that you had devised your own way of appeasing me."

He shook his head as he quickly stepped forward to place his hands on her shoulders. "It's not like that, sweetheart."

"Don't call me that." Jerking from his grasp, her shaky voice rose considerably as she fought to keep her emotions in check. "Don't ever call me that again."

"Dammit, Alyssa, listen to me."

"Why should I? You haven't been honest with me thus far, why should I believe you now?"

"You have to calm down and see reason."

Struggling to keep the torrent of tears in check just a few moments longer, she glared at him. "I don't *have* to do anything but leave, Mr. Walker. And that's exactly what I intend to do."

Her legs felt as if they might not support her as she walked over to pick up the small overnight case she'd packed when they'd stopped by her apartment the evening before. Heading down the hall, she stopped at the first bedroom she came to, quickly changed out of his shirt and into her own clothes, then called a cab.

When she walked out into the hall, Caleb was waiting for her. He'd changed into a chambray shirt, worn jeans and scuffed boots.

If he thought reverting to his good-old-boy persona would make a difference, he was sadly mistaken. "Excuse me," she said, starting to walk past him. "I'll wait outside for my ride."

He stood stock still. "I'll drive you back to Albuquerque."

"No, you won't."

Folding his arms across his wide chest, he looked dubious. "Then how do you expect to get back home?"

"If I have to, I'll walk." She brushed past him. "But that's no longer any of your concern, Mr. Walker."

"Don't be so damned stubborn that you do something foolish," he said, following her down the hall to the front door.

When she turned on him, her body trembled with a

combination of anger and emotional pain. "We've already established that I cornered the market on foolishness."

Opening the door, she walked out and slammed it behind her. As she hurried down the driveway, she remembered that she'd left Sidney's cage in the family room. But she couldn't go back for the parakeet. She'd have to call later and request that Caleb bring the bird to the office.

Right now, she needed to put as much distance as she could between herself and Caleb. If she went back, he'd realize that she'd fallen hopelessly in love with him. And that was something she'd rather die than have him do.

Caleb stood watch until Alyssa got into the cab, then, turning away from the window, he walked out onto the patio. Everything inside him shouted for him to go after her, to bring her back and make her listen to reason, to convince her to hear what he had to say. But she was hurting right now and just knowing that he was the cause of it tied him in knots.

He'd had every intention of telling Alyssa about himself last night. But when they'd gone into the bedroom, he'd been so hot for her again that they'd made love until they'd both fallen asleep from complete exhaustion. Then he'd planned as soon as he finished his shower to serve her breakfast in bed, tell her everything, then ask her to make their engagement real.

But, Emerald had beaten him to it. That complicated

matters greatly, but it didn't mean he was ready to throw in the towel.

Alyssa needed time to calm down. And he needed time to make a few plans.

If there was one thing he'd inherited from his paternal grandmother, it was her determination. The old gal hadn't gotten where she was today without it and he fully intended to use her legacy to win back the only woman he'd ever love.

Ten

Alyssa sniffed back a fresh wave of tears as she sat on her couch, staring at her apartment walls. She'd expected Caleb to call on Monday after finding her resignation on his desk, along with a request that he leave Sidney in Geneva's care. But by close of business Wednesday, she realized that he didn't care about her leaving Skerritt and Crowe. And it was apparent he didn't intend to return her bird.

"The least he could have done was give Sidney back to me," she muttered miserably.

When the doorbell rang, she sighed. It was probably Mrs. Rogers again. The older woman had been sweeping her walk Saturday morning when Alyssa had gotten out of the cab and, taking one look at Alyssa's red-rimmed eyes, the woman had decided to lend moral support. She'd been over at least twice a day since, and today it appeared that she was going to make it three times.

Getting up from the couch, she walked over to open the door. "I'm fine, Mrs.—" She stopped abruptly. "You aren't Mrs. Rogers."

The red-haired, freckle-faced young man in a white courier's uniform grinned and shook his head. "Afraid not." He glanced at the clipboard in his hand. "Are you Ms. Alyssa Jane Merrick?"

"Yes."

"I have an express for you," he said, handing her an envelope marked Urgent. "Could you please sign on line twenty-four?"

Signing where the young man indicated, she started to thank him, but he was already halfway back to his delivery truck. When he squealed the tires as he pulled away from the curb, she decided that he took the company's claim of being the speediest delivery service in the world a little too seriously.

As she closed the door, she glanced at the return address. Who on earth did she know in Wichita, Kansas?

Her heart suddenly stopped, then started hammering at her throat. Emerald, Inc.'s headquarters were in Wichita.

Her hands shook as Alyssa pulled the tab to open the thin cardboard packet. If Emerald Larson had sent anything but a final paycheck, she'd get it back so fast she'd wonder if it had ever left her office.

But when Alyssa pulled the papers out of the envelope and thumbed through them, her mouth fell open. It was her letter of resignation, along with a handwritten note from Emerald Larson, herself.

Dearest Alyssa,

In order for your resignation as operations manager of Skerritt and Crowe Financial Consultants to be effective, you'll need to deliver it to me in person. I've arranged for a car to pick you up at your apartment tomorrow morning at eight. Please be prompt. The corporate jet will be waiting to fly you to Wichita, then return you to Albuquerque later in the day.

Yours truly,

Emerald Larson

Suddenly feeling as if her knees were made of jelly, Alyssa sat on the couch to stare at the letter. She'd never heard of anyone having to hand deliver their resignation. Why would the woman do that? Was it even legal for Emerald Larson to require that of her?

Alyssa wasn't sure. But she'd go to Wichita if that was what it took to divorce herself from Skerritt and Crowe, Emerald, Inc. and the fiasco with Caleb. Then she'd spend the rest of her life trying to forget the only man she would ever love.

"Who's your mole at Skerritt and Crowe, Emerald?" Caleb sat in the executive office of Emerald, Inc., staring across the French provincial desk at his indomitable grandmother. "And don't tell me you don't know what I'm talking about. You had to have someone at the firm feeding you information. Otherwise, you wouldn't have mentioned that Alyssa and I make a good team."

To her credit, she didn't even try to pretend that she didn't know what he was talking about. "Does it matter, darling?"

"Yes, it does." He wasn't about to let her get away with playing her little mind games. "You told me, Hunter and Nick that we'd have free reign in managing the companies you gave us—*without* your interference."

"I haven't interfered with the way you're running the financial firm." She smiled. "I just wanted to keep track of how you're doing, that's all."

"Did it ever occur to you to ask me?"

She patted a platinum hair back into place. "I wanted an unbiased opinion."

Caleb sat forward. "Let me assure you. If I'm about to land on my ass, I'll let you know so you can send in one of your ace managers to clean up the mess before it's too late. I'm not about to let the employees at Skerritt and Crowe pay the price for my screwups. They're good people and I don't want to see them hurt by your little experiment."

Instead of being offended by his statement, the old gal looked as pleased as punch. "All right."

"And I'll tell you something else." If she thought he was finished, she was sadly mistaken. "If I find out you're playing any more of your little games with me or the firm, I'm out. I'll go back to Tennessee and you can forget offering me any more of your sweet deals because I'll turn them down flat."

To his surprise, she grinned. "I would expect no less from a grandson of mine." She glanced at the diamond-encrusted watch on her left wrist. "Alyssa should be arriving in just a few moments. Are you sure you don't want me to stay? I might be able to clarify the facts about your father."

He shook his head. "You're getting her here was enough. I'll handle it from here on out."

She stood up and walked toward the door. "If you need me—"

"I won't." Too keyed up to remain seated, he rose to his feet. If he had any chance of a future with Alyssa, he had to be completely honest with her. And the information about himself would have to come from him, not his rich-as-sin grandmother. "I got myself into this. I'll get myself out."

Emerald nodded approvingly. "I hope your young

woman realizes what a good man you are, Caleb. Best of luck, son."

Caleb stared at her for several long moments. There was a sincerity in her voice that he hadn't expected. "Thank you…Grandmother."

When Alyssa stepped off the elevator on the sixth floor of Emerald Towers, a distinguished-looking gentleman of about fifty was waiting for her. "Ms. Merrick, please follow me. I'm Mrs. Larson's personal assistant, Luther Freemont. I've been instructed to take you directly to her private office."

As she followed the man down a long hall, Alyssa clutched the folder containing her resignation. She wasn't nervous, but she was eager to get her meeting with Emerald Larson over with. Once she'd done that, she could work on rebuilding her life.

Mr. Freemont stopped in front of a set of tall, ornately carved mahogany doors. Holding one of them open for her, he stepped back. "I hope your meeting turns out to everyone's satisfaction, Ms. Merrick."

"Thank you."

Why would the man tell her something like that? Was Mrs. Larson going to try to talk her out of resigning?

If so, the woman was in for a disappointment. There was no way Alyssa could continue working at the firm as long as Caleb was there.

But when she walked into the office, her heart felt as

if it had dropped to the floor. Instead of finding Emerald Larson in the plush executive office, she saw Caleb looking out the plate-glass window.

When he turned to face her, he looked so devastatingly handsome that her breath caught and a shaft of longing went straight to her soul. His low-slung jeans emphasized his lean waist and muscular thighs, while the knit fabric of his navy polo shirt drew attention to the well-developed muscles of his upper body, reminding her of how strong he was, how easily he'd held her when they'd made love in the shower. His light brown hair was slightly mussed as if he'd recently run his hand through it, but it only added to his appeal.

"Good morning, Alyssa."

"Where's Mrs. Larson?"

He shrugged. "I suppose she's around the offices here somewhere."

His smile and the sound of his deep Southern drawl caused a wave of emotion so strong it threatened to bend her double, to sweep through her. She turned to leave. "I can't do this," she whispered.

"Wait, Alyssa." He quickly crossed the room to take hold of her upper arms. "Please, I need for you to hear what I have to say. Then, if you still want to resign, I promise I won't try to stop you."

"Is this the only way you'll accept my resignation?" she asked, already knowing his answer.

"I'm afraid so, sweetheart." He turned her to face

him, then stepped back and motioned toward a sitting area by the doors. "Have a seat."

"I'd rather not."

"This may take a while."

She shook her head. "Caleb, I don't really think there's any point in—"

He folded his arms over his wide chest. "I do."

Suddenly feeling completely defeated, she walked over to sit down on the edge of one of the overstuffed armchairs. She stared at the folder on her lap. "Please make this quick."

He was silent for a moment and she could tell he was waiting for her to look at him. But she couldn't. If she did, she knew without question she'd fall apart.

"Everything I told you about myself is true, Alyssa," he said quietly. "I grew up on a farm in central Tennessee and I have two brothers—Hunter O'Banyon and Nick Daniels." He hesitated as if he didn't like what he had to say next. "I've never lied to you. But I am guilty of omitting a few facts."

"B-but you did lie to me," she said, hating that her voice shook with emotion. She looked at him directly. "You told me you went to the University of Tennessee."

He smiled sadly and shook his head. "I said there was no other team like the UT Vols. I never said I attended classes there."

"But you knew what I'd think."

Nodding, he ran his hand over the back of his neck.

"I'm not proud of that. But it was easier to let you draw your own conclusions than it was to admit that I have nothing more than a high-school education."

His expression grim, he sat on the end of the coffee table in front of her. When she noticed their knees were almost touching, she scooted back in the chair. If he touched her in any way, she feared she'd lose the tenuous hold she had on her feelings.

She watched him prop his forearms on his thighs and stare down at his loosely clasped hands. "I had an academic scholarship to go to UT at Knoxville, but I had to turn it down. Grandpa got sick that summer and I was needed at home to keep the farm going. Then later on, it was a matter of economics."

There was deep regret in his tone and she could tell that his lack of a postsecondary education bothered him a lot. "There's still time to get your degree."

He shrugged. "I'm enrolled in night classes for the fall semester."

She frowned. Something didn't add up. "Now, hold it. Emerald Larson is your grandmother. Why couldn't she have helped you out with school?"

"It wasn't until last month that my brothers and I learned about each other and that we're the product of the late Owen Larson sowing his wild oats." He laughed humorlessly. "Until then, we didn't have a clue who our father was or that we were related to one of the richest women in the world."

"You're kidding."

"I wish I was joking," he said, shaking his head. "But unfortunately, I'm not."

She couldn't begin to imagine what a shock that must have been for the three men. "How did you find out?"

"Luther Freemont showed up at the farm one day to tell me that I was needed in Wichita." He looked as if he still had trouble believing it himself. "When I asked him who was making the request and why, he said he wasn't at liberty to tell me. So, I told him to go to hell and went back to working on my tractor."

"I take it he didn't give up?"

Caleb shook his head. "My mom stepped in and told me that it was time to learn about my father and that she wanted me to go."

"I don't understand," Alyssa said, wondering why it had been such a big secret. All things considered, she shouldn't care. But she could see that he'd been deeply affected by what had taken place and she couldn't stop herself from asking, "Why hadn't she told you who your father was?"

"That's where it gets complicated." Taking a deep breath, he added, "Emerald Larson knew about all of us, practically from the moment we were conceived. But she didn't want us turning out like her son—our father."

"So she didn't acknowledge any of you until recently?" Alyssa couldn't understand how Emerald Larson could live in the lap of luxury while denying her grandsons the opportunities that would have made their lives easier.

He shook his head. "She told us that she knew she'd made a lot of mistakes when she gave Owen everything he wanted, instead of giving him the time and attention he needed from her. She said she also knew that we'd have a better chance of turning out to be decent men if our lifestyle was more down-to-earth and we were raised by mothers who taught us the values that she'd failed to teach Owen." He smiled. "As crazy as it sounds, Emerald was actually trying to protect us."

Alyssa thought about it for a moment. "I guess, in a strange way, that makes sense." She shook her head. "But it doesn't explain why your mother failed to tell you about your father."

His expression turned dark. "I'm still having a problem with this part of the whole sordid mess. Mom worked at one of the luxury hotels in Nashville. She was a young, naive country girl and Owen swept her off her feet. Then after he left town, Emerald contacted Mom through a private investigator while she was pregnant and arranged to support us with a modest monthly allowance. The only requirement was that Mom couldn't tell anyone—including me—who my father was. Emerald even went so far as to have Mom sign a legal agreement stating that if she divulged who had gotten her pregnant that I would be cut out of inheriting any part of Emerald, Inc. and the Larson fortune. She did the same thing with Hunter's and Nick's mothers."

Alyssa could understand Mrs. Larson's not wanting the boys to turn out like their father. No one in their right mind would want to see a child grow up to be a hedonistic, irresponsible adult, which she'd heard Owen Larson had been before the boating accident that had claimed his life six months ago. But what Caleb was describing that Emerald Larson had required of the women sounded suspiciously like blackmail.

"And in all that time, your mother never told anyone who your father was?"

His intense gaze met hers. "No. She felt that she was ensuring a better future for me than she could ever give me on her own."

Alyssa couldn't help but be a bit envious. Her mother had loved and doted on her when she'd been alive, but after her death, Alyssa hadn't felt that she'd been loved by anyone.

They remained silent for several long moments before he took a deep breath. "When we all arrived in Wichita and Emerald explained about our father and that she was going to give each of us one of her companies to run, I fully intended to turn her down because I didn't feel qualified to run a place like Skerritt and Crowe."

"What changed your mind?"

"I thought about my mom's dream of giving me a better life and I knew I had to give it a try." He shrugged.

"So I started reading books on management and went on the Internet to search for everything I could about creating a better work atmosphere and unity among the workers. Then I remembered seeing a report on one of the news shows a year or so back about companies using innovative ways to keep employees motivated. I bought a couple of books, did a little more research on the computer and the changes I've made at Skerritt and Crowe are the result."

"It worked." Her conscience wouldn't allow her to say otherwise. "Everyone at the firm is a lot happier than they were under the old management."

He shrugged. "I also figured if I made it a nice place to work, left everyone alone to do their jobs and let you make the business decisions, I'd be okay until I could take some administrative courses and get an idea of what I was really supposed to be doing."

His admission caused her chest to tighten and she wasn't sure she'd be able to draw her next breath. Thinking he'd been using her was one thing, but hearing him put it into words hurt more than she could have ever imagined.

"I—I really need…to go." She quickly stood up and shoved the file containing her resignation into his hands. If she didn't get out of there soon the floodgates were going to open. "G-good luck with…the firm."

Rising to his feet, he tossed the folder to the floor and pulled her into his arms. "I haven't told you the most important detail of all, Alyssa."

He cradled her close and the feel of his strong arms folded around her, the wide expanse of his chest pillowing her head, and the tender way he stroked her hair caused her heart to break even more. Just knowing that once she walked out the door she'd never again be held by him or know the softness of his kiss was almost more than she could bear.

"C-Caleb, p-please—"

"Don't cry, sweetheart. It tears me apart to see you cry." His chest rose and fell beneath her ear as he took a deep shuddering breath. "Do you want to know what happened when I arrived at Skerritt and Crowe?"

"N-no."

"I fell in love with a beautiful, intelligent woman who tried to hide how wonderful she is behind baggy suits and oversize glasses." Leaning back, he cupped her face with his large hands and the sincerity she saw in his incredible hazel gaze caused her heart to skip several beats. "Yes, I let you call the shots at the firm. But I never used you. I never took credit for anything."

As she stared up at him, she realized that what he'd said was true. The main reason everyone at Skerritt and Crowe was so happy was the fact that Caleb left them alone to do their jobs and didn't try to micromanage their every move.

"I—I'm sorry that I jumped to conclusions." She took a deep, steadying breath. It was suddenly important that he understand why she'd refused to listen to him that morning, how she'd let fear blind her to the facts. "Before I came to work at the firm, I made a huge mistake by getting involved with a coworker who used our relationship to gain information about a client I had been hoping to sign. He took all the credit for the research and winning the account, then got a promotion for all of *his* hard work."

"The jerk should be shot for doing that to you." Caleb shook his head. "No wonder you thought I'd been using you to make myself look good."

"I suppose in a way, I was looking for it to happen." Her voice caught. "I guess I expected for you to hurt me the same way he had."

His intense gaze held hers. "Do you still feel that way, Alyssa?"

"No." Caleb may have omitted a couple of important facts, but he had told her as much as he could about himself without revealing who his grandmother was and that he didn't have the credentials to run Skerritt and Crowe.

Caleb kissed her temple. "I love you, Alyssa Jane Merrick. Never doubt that. And I'd never do anything to hurt you, sweetheart."

"I know that now." Her eyes filled with moisture, but this time they were tears of joy. "I…love you, too, Caleb. So very much."

He crushed her to him, kissing her until they both gasped for breath. "I want to spend the rest of my life proving to you just how much you mean to me, sweetheart." Stepping back, he pulled a small velvet box from his jeans pocket and removed a diamond-and-sapphire ring from inside. Then, dropping to one knee, he took her left hand in his. "Alyssa, will you marry me?"

Her heart filled with so much love it felt as if it would burst. "Yes."

Slipping the ring on her finger, he rose to take her into his arms. "I intend to spend the rest of my life making sure you never regret becoming my wife, sweetheart."

She wrapped her arms around his waist. "I could never regret marrying the only man I'll ever love."

"God, I missed you," he said, kissing her eyes, her cheeks and the tip of her nose. "And I wasn't the only one."

"I missed you, too." She leaned back to look at him. "What do you mean you weren't the only one?"

Caleb laughed. "Sidney missed you, too."

Grinning, she asked, "Why didn't you return him?"

His sexy grin caused her stomach to flutter. "I had every intention of holding him hostage for as long as it took to get you to say yes."

"There was no way I would have said otherwise." She glanced at the ring on the third finger of her left hand. "How did you know what size of ring I wear?"

He shook his head. "I don't know how Emerald does it, but after I picked out the ring I wanted to give you, she told me she'd take care of having it sized."

"But we'd only spoken on the phone, she's never met me. How did she know?"

"I'm not sure, but she has her ways. Now, let's introduce the two of you, then head for the airport." He took her hand in his and led her to the door. "We have something waiting for us back at my house."

"And what would that be?"

Caleb's sexy grin sent waves of heat coursing through every cell in her body. "A hot tub."

"I like the way you think." Raising up on tiptoe, she kissed his lean cheek. "I love you with all my heart, Caleb Walker."

His tender smile lit the darkest corners of her soul. "I love you, too, Alyssa Jane Merrick. Now, let's go home and I'll get started on that lifetime promise of showing you just how much."

Epilogue

"How much longer?" Caleb asked, walking over to gaze out the farmhouse window.

"I swear to God if you don't stop pacing, Hunter and I are going to tie you down," Nick said, laughing.

Hunter checked his watch. "You have approximately fifteen minutes of freedom left, bro." Grinning, he slapped Caleb on the shoulder. "There's still time to make a run for it."

Caleb shook his head. "No way. Alyssa's everything I've ever wanted."

"You're one lucky son of a gun," Nick said, smiling. "She's a great girl."

"Nick and I both wish you the best," Hunter added

as they headed for the door. "When is she taking over the reins at the financial firm?"

"Right after we get back from our honeymoon in the Bahamas." Caleb led the way toward the meadow down by the creek. "Our plan is for her to keep things going until I get my business degree, then we'll run it together."

"And Emerald is okay with that?" Nick asked, looking doubtful.

"She's the one who suggested it," Caleb said, taking his place beside the preacher from the local Methodist church.

As he gazed over the small crowd seated in white folding chairs under the shade of the oak tree he'd climbed as a boy, he noticed that several of the Skerritt and Crowe employees had made the trip from New Mexico to Tennessee for the wedding. His smile widened when his gaze drifted to his mother and grandmothers. On opposite sides of the aisle, they were chatting congenially. All things considered, he'd have never believed it was possible, but his mother, his grandma Walker and Emerald had become fairly good friends.

His heart swelled with love for the women in his life. When he'd brought Alyssa home to meet his mother and grandmother, they'd immediately accepted her as the daughter and granddaughter they'd never had. Then, to his surprise, his mother had called Emerald and the four of them had had a grand old time planning the wedding together.

But when the string quartet that Emerald had insisted on hiring started playing "Here Comes the Bride" and the crowd rose to their feet, Caleb turned his attention to the woman being escorted down the aisle by Malcolm Fuller. Alyssa was dressed in a long, white, satin-and-lace wedding gown, and he'd never seen her look more beautiful. Her gaze never wavered from his and, when Malcolm put her hand in Caleb's, her radiant smile lit the darkest corners of his soul.

"I love you, sweetheart. Are you ready to become Mrs. Walker?"

"I've been waiting for this moment my entire life," she whispered.

"They make a very striking couple," Emerald murmured, watching Caleb raise Alyssa's veil.

"Quite," Luther Freemont agreed.

As she watched her handsome grandson kiss his lovely bride, Emerald smiled. She'd been right to pair Caleb with Alyssa. From the first time she'd spoken on the phone with the young woman, Emerald had been impressed with her intelligence and business acumen. Then, after a discreet check into Alyssa's background, she'd instinctively known each was exactly what the other needed. Caleb was a natural-born leader and Alyssa a sensitive intellect. They were a perfect match and together they would be a major force to contend with in the financial world, not to mention producing beautiful, intelligent heirs.

Extremely pleased with the results of her first endeavor, she turned her attention to her other two grandsons. Hunter and Nick were going to be a challenge. Both of them had pasts that would have to be overcome before they could find their happiness.

But she wasn't worried. She and Luther had done their research and had put their plans into action. In the months to come, she fully expected everything to turn out to her satisfaction with Hunter and Nick as well.

When Caleb and Alyssa walked down the aisle as husband and wife, Emerald turned to Luther with a smug smile. "One down and two to go."

* * * * *

COMING NEXT MONTH

#1705 TAKING CARE OF BUSINESS—Brenda Jackson
The Elliotts
How far will an Elliott heir go to convince a working-class woman that passion is color-blind?

#1706 TEMPT ME—Caroline Cross
Men of Steele
He is the hunter. She is his prey. And he's out to catch her at any cost.

#1707 REUNION OF REVENGE—Kathie DeNosky
The Illegitimate Heirs
Once run off the ranch, this millionaire now owns it…along with the woman who was nearly his undoing.

#1708 HIS WEDDING-NIGHT WAGER—Katherine Garbera
What Happens in Vegas…
She left him standing at the altar. Now this jilted groom is hell-bent on having his revenge…and a wedding night!

#1709 SEVEN-YEAR SEDUCTION—Heidi Betts
Would one week together be enough to satisfy a seduction seven years in the making?

#1710 SURROGATE AND WIFE—Emily McKay
She was only supposed to have the baby…not *marry* the father of her surrogate child.

SDCNM0106